Captains Wanted

CAPTAINS WANTED

A NOVEL

ANDRES SCHABELMAN

NEW YORK

LONDON • NASHVILLE • MELBOURNE • VANCOUVER

Captains Wanted

A Novel

Published in New York, New York, by Morgan James Publishing. Morgan James is a trademark of Morgan James, LLC. www.MorganJamesPublishing.com

Proudly distributed by Publishers Group West®

Publisher's Note: This novel is a work of fiction. Names, characters, places, and incidents are either products of the author's imagination or used fictitiously. All characters are fictional, and any similarity to people living or dead is purely coincidental.

Morgan James BOGO™

A **FREE** ebook edition is available for you or a friend with the purchase of this print book.

CLEARLY SIGN YOUR NAME ABOVE

Instructions to claim your free ebook edition:
1. Visit MorganJamesBOGO.com
2. Sign your name CLEARLY in the space above
3. Complete the form and submit a photo of this entire page
4. You or your friend can download the ebook to your preferred device

ISBN 9781636984384 paperback
ISBN 9781636984391 ebook
Library of Congress Control Number: 2024933231

Cover & Interior Design by:
Christopher Kirk
www.GFSstudio.com

Morgan James PUBLISHING

Builds

with...

Habitat for Humanity® Peninsula and Greater Williamsburg

Morgan James is a proud partner of Habitat for Humanity Peninsula and Greater Williamsburg. Partners in building since 2006.

Get involved today! Visit: www.morgan-james-publishing.com/giving-back

To Al "Dweez" Dwyer and Aaron Pinsky, both who have guided this book in this reality and in some other realms as well.

Pinsky, your last words, "I am the captain of this ship," (and your entire much-too-short time on this planet) obviously live on inside of me and this book.

And Al, you are me and I am you, and I am forever thankful for this journey of life we continue to be on.

May these words that follow provide the mirror to return back to our higher selves and allow us to be the instruments of balance this chaotic yet beautiful world needs.

CONTENTS

BUT FIRST, THE MAP

write these words amid a storm. Rain batters the wood that protects me. Wind howls. Panes of glass rattle and beams creak. A wall of layered gray clouds covers the sky overhead. I have to lean in my chair and twist my neck to see the only places where the storm is torn open. There, behind dangling threads of fog, do the tiniest blue patches peek out from the other side. In only one place, for only the briefest interval, can I see where the sun turns one cloud lump as bright white as a lampshade.

Most novels come with prologues, and most non-fiction books with introductions. Other books prefer the classic, "Once upon a time" or "In the beginning," but what best serves us is to meet where we are. Only there, wherever that is, will we connect and journey together, whatever the weather. In other words, we need a map. Since I don't have a map for you, we'll have to share one.

Since you are in the storm with me—or rather, we are both in the same storm—let's roll out this map and have a looksee. Imagine as we fold it out over the table, how the edges are so worn from use or age, or both, that we have to put paperweights down on each of the corners. We notice some words along the frayed bottom edge. They read:

"Let's pretend you are me and I am you. The two of us are going to see a play unfold, but it's a play in book form. Remember, that wordplay has two meanings: as a theatrical performance and as something we freely enjoy without taking it so seriously. Like child's play. Let's each use whichever meaning of play works for us. All of these words, in fact, this entire map, like all maps, is merely navigation instructions about how to best enjoy the performance—and by that, of course, we mean how to best participate in it."

Let's set the record straight here. We can all agree that maps are better when illustrated with a sense of ratios and space and distance, a tool with which to orient ourselves visually. The kind of thing our direction-oriented side, what people often unfairly call the *masculine side of us*, craves. You know, the kind that gives us an overview of where the book will take us, complete with little drawings and labels and danger signs. It appears this map consists only of words. This raises questions. Many of them.

What's the point of writing a map instead of drawing one?

We thought this was a book, but now we are being told it's a play that requires a map and a set of instructions? Aren't these mixed forms? Are we going to get a user manual next? What the Matryoshka-nesting-doll is going on here?

Besides, how can we have any idea what it's like to be someone else?

And who are we, really, anyway?

Thankfully, the map has some answers. Toward the top, there is a block of text. It says:

"It seems people want to believe there are secrets, keys, gurus, principals, values, affirmations, lessons, or other short lists that become foolproof recipes for *success*—whatever that word is supposed to mean. We're told to live out our passions. We're told to follow our dreams. We're also told that the rent is going up, that being alive is expensive, that being sick is expensive, and that even dying isn't afford-able. For this reason, most of us are imprisoned, pushed and pulled by a sense of scarcity. We're not operating from the heart. The heart, we're told, isn't good for business. But the heart is good for life. It *is* life. And life, as it turns out, is good for everything. Even business. And that's why, one day, just after receiving another message from someone soliciting my advice, I was relieved to find this book, once lost among my possessions. It had been hiding, spine pointed inward, in a bookcase. I vaguely recog-nized the book, like maybe it was something from a dream."

OK, so it seems this map is part of the book itself. A legend, we might call it, if that word resonates. We feel like this is already a bit much. Books don't usually come with these sorts of bizarre instructions, and it starts to feel like it's more trouble than it's worth. We look up from the map for a moment. Outside, the pounding rain has weakened to a misty spray. As we watch the weather change, our hand brushes against the paperweight holding the bottom right-hand corner. It topples over. When we move to fix it, we notice it has concealed some other words. Here they are:

"When I held its soothing, furry cover in my hands, I was overcome by a warm sensation. It was an intu-itive sense that the book would add value to some-one else's life. At first, this was an absurd idea. After all, I had never read it myself; how could I know it could help someone else? That's why I cracked it open and began to read. Soon, I discovered something else—something that surprised me in a way I can't exactly describe. Not with language anyway."

Welp. That's not exactly helpful. If this map is relying on language, and all we have are words telling us words aren't going to cut it, that leaves us a bit adrift. Or maybe we prefer the term, "out at sea?" We follow our eyes up to the top right-hand corner, where we remove the paperweight and find more words waiting for us. See:

"I'm sure you must have questions; many whom I've shared this book with have. Where did it come from? Who wrote it? And why? Is it fiction? Is it real? Or at least based on a true story? I cannot give any definitive answers here, but your most pressing questions will be resolved over the course of reading what follows. Or they won't. That's life too. For now, what I can say is this is the book you've been waiting for. The one that could guide you to your perfect job. The one that might help you nail the interview. The one that will show you how to bask in the good life that your dream job affords. It will also show you a way out, offering a respite in this modern, confusing world. What you're holding is the lighthouse on how to find your wind, even create your waves, and it will direct you to steer your vessel a certain way. *This way.*"

Now we're more curious. We notice something else too. The weather has changed again. We glance up to see the patch of blue sky has expanded. It's covering almost a quarter of the sky now and is spreading rapidly. The wind has lessened to a breeze, and the rain has stopped. The storm is passing. Soon, we can venture outside. We could even roll this map up and save it for some other time. We consider this as we gaze outside. The light keeps shifting. The sun appears for one moment and then is concealed once more behind a cloud.

On second thought, the weather doesn't seem like it's quite made up its mind. It could go either way. In the meantime, we lift the paperweight from the top left corner as a debate brews inside, threatening to separate us back into our separate selves.

What have we got to lose by reading it?

But we doubt the words.

So do we. So go right ahead and doubt them.

Come on, who doesn't need a beacon to brave the waters of life?

With doubt the only victor in the debate, we read the following passage hidden below the third paperweight:

"I've been asked by many for career advice. No matter how often this happens, I always find it strange. I barely know what it's like to be me. How can I have any idea what it's like to be you? What's the point of me theorizing about what you might or might not do differently to live or change your life? The only advice I will give you is this: be prepared to let go of "I" and get into "you." In fact, the whole book is written like this. Sure, there are characters, but they are all me, which means they are all you. Even AI, a supposed collaborator. I mean, is he a real person or another name for AI? Capital A. Capital I. Even I'm not sure. I can only apologize in advance for the ways I might show up inauthentically. While the "I" to "you" transition is one I am asking you to make for the purpose of you stepping into You, I recognize it isn't without the desired outcome of self-sovereignty. Still, I hope you will forgive me and use this as a practice, if only to watch and learn how the parts of you or the parts of our external surroundings impose their views on you."

With just one paperweight left to remove, we find that all of this feels easier said than done. It has started to sound like a project better left imagined than actually brought to life. We wonder whether the map itself—and the book and play that it is supposed to help us navigate this road—is better left rolled up nice and tight and stowed deeply away in the hull, wherever that is. Sunlight pours through the curtains, beckoning us away from the page. We wonder whether it's even worth lifting up the last paperweight. Whatever the book holds, it seems like it would be at least a bit of a drag. But then we look down to see the paperweight is already gone, revealing the final words on the map:

"That's right, the performance can seem like a bit of a drag at some junctures. But it's a short, easy read. That's intentional. This is an effort to give more life, not take it away. And remember, the answers are all within us anyway, and if we were ever to need additional pages, head outdoors like we want to, jump into the water, or sit under a tree, and listen, we can. We just might be able to write more pages ourselves. We can burn a couple of hours between these pages, or we can burn them by binge-watching a new show or by burning the book itself. It's our choice. But something tells me we are the keepers of human connection. Something tells me we can save the world. Something tells me this map shows the way."

With that, the map rolls back into itself and disappears. *Woosh.* Nothing remains, like a deleted letter on a Word document. Outside, the storm is gone too. All that remains is a book in your hands and a pair of questions without askers.

What if we really are the keepers of human connection?

Ready?

We aren't either. Again, it's okay. Here's a toast to our success and our journey. Good luck. We can't wait to hear all about it.

CHAPTER 1

FAKE IT UNTIL YOU DON'T MAKE IT

A t last, the madness is over. You made it. You're here.

A pair of large windows frame the city like a postcard. The room is warm. Art hangs on the walls with a comforting plainness. Your guts rumble with the act of getting here, but the worst is over.

Because you've arrived.

There is, of course, more to it than that. Credit is due. People helped because you leveraged your contacts. You submitted your application and your cover letter and added that light tap-tap on the old digital doorknocker of a certain manager. You do owe some credit to the circumstances that conspired in your favor to get you here, waiting for the glass of water you were offered—and eagerly accepted based on that yes-to-everything mentality that's gotten you *here, now*—and that you hope will keep you lubricated enough to slide out answers to the impending questions, just like you practiced at home this morning. And as you slept. And last night. And the day before that.

Be calm and confident, you coach yourself. *Act natural, like this is no biggie.*

Soon, the chair across the glass table from you will be filled. The moment of reckoning will arrive. You will finally unbuckle yourself and step out into your new life.

You graduated from college several years ago and, right away, hopped on the first career roller coaster, which led to another. And another. And a third—until now, this moment, where you plan to put all the funny business behind you at last. Fool you thrice and that's once too many.

For a moment, you imagine your parents sitting on the couch against the edge of the room between the windows. They've watched you, cheered for you, and smiled at you as you've twisted and turned, rose and plummeted, sometimes at breakneck speeds, other times at slow-motion crawls. Clinks and whooshes. Splashes and whirrs. Whenever your face met theirs on this journey, their eyes were filled with joy, wonder, and pride. Their smiles are burned into your memory, more than any section of the track ever could be, more than any employee recognition or happy hour special or project success.

But now their demeanor has changed. Mom shakes her head. Dad gazes downward. They can tell you're nervous.

From your perspective, today should be another chance for them to collect one more badge of honor to display to their friends and extended family. For you, it's an opportunity to show them you've finally earned the right to feel like your feet are planted on solid ground with a job you actually want. A job that will challenge you, reward you, maybe define you.

You've read the books. You've rehearsed the techniques. You've mapped out the path and factored in its risks and rewards. It's all correct. Being accepted for the interview felt like a matter of natural law. It feels right to be here.

The assistant arrives with the water.

"Just one more thing." Your words are slow and calculated. "How do I pronounce her last name, exactly?"

"Xuan," the assistant says. "Like *shoe* and *Juan* are jammed together. Shoe-Juan. *Xuan.*"

"Shuan."

She nods. You thank her. She leaves.

You sip. You wait. You feel your tummy region bubble a bit again, and just like that, you decide not to try to pronounce her name at all. It's too risky and today is not the day to roll the dice.

This isn't just the dream job. This isn't just the dream company. This isn't just about perfect timing. This is all of those things combined with the secret sauce on top. This is also your dream city. This is where you see your future. This is the plan in action. You've manifested it.

Over the last few years, you've endured a few more rickety rides than you'd expected. But you smiled at your parents, and at those other onlookers, mustering a way to mirror their jubilation no matter how much pain the sudden turns, rock-hard seats, and unsafe speeds caused you. Before you got on each ride, of course, you had no idea they were roller coasters in the amusement park of life. Each time, you thought it was more like a spa—a place you'd been encouraged to enter by the over-ecstatic staff welcoming you in. These were all places you were supposed to enjoy, where you were supposed to be happy.

But what you thought was a door handle was really just a seatbelt on another roller coaster.

All the same, you put up with the nonsense. You took on the responsibilities of your colleagues when they slacked off. You embraced company culture even when it was flawed, even when you had to wear silly hats, sing songs with lyrics you didn't believe in, and pledge allegiance to flags you knew were on fire. You did what it took to keep advancing. You closed your eyes and endured. You managed to avoid passing out. You didn't vomit, not even when you really wanted to—when you needed to. You swallowed it all back down and kept your momentum.

As you draw near to what you're sure, this time, must be a doorway to somewhere more peaceful, those somersaults in your belly are just excitement about finally being at the right place, at the right time.

Right?

"You must have been thirsty," she says when she finally walks in.

The glass in your hand is already more than half empty. You set it down on the cork coaster with a soft thud. You stand and shake her hand.

"I guess I was." You chuckle even as your insides shriek excitedly, a mix of giddiness and nerves.

She doesn't sit in the chair so much as glide into it. The wheels slide across the wooden floor until her knees bump into her desk, effectively stopping her right in front of you. Her dress is minimal and to the point. Her hair has a playfulness, but the overall message is not in doubt. She is a competent leader, the kind you want to be.

She'll be fun to work for. And she'll make a great mentor.

You played it right down the middle with your wardrobe—nothing too tight or too loose, too formal or too casual, too colorful or too bland. You give nothing away with what you're wearing. Your resumé is supposed to do that—and you're thrilled to see it is the only thing besides her confidence that she's brought into the room. Well, that and the first-class ticket to the future you were told, just this morning on a phone call with your mother, that you deserve. Dad reminded you that you've earned it. It's a future you're all ready for.

"Your resume had a big, bright sticky note on it," she begins. "Seems someone around here really wants you onboard."

You smile just enough, shrug your shoulders, and play it off like a humble person. You're the kind of person who can take themselves just seriously enough. You want her to see that. You want her to feel that. You want her to want to work together.

She asks about your last gig, the roller coaster you had only recently wobbled off, thanks to this interview. You had to leave it behind. The only reward for remaining would have been a lifetime of mediocrity, a story you never wanted to live, a journey without a final destination. Career development gurus have long outlined the two paths. Some places have ceilings. That place did; this place does not. Some people have ceilings.

She does not. You hope you are in the same category. A reading of the experts on the topic suggests you might be, but now you have to prove it, to check the boxes in her mind—and by extension, everyone's minds.

You don't tell her any of this, obviously. You talk in terms of "challenges" and "objectives." You speak about "trajectory" and "moving the needle." You pepper in just enough "disruptor" and "innovation" talk, without overdoing it.

She takes it all in. Nodding. Smiling. There's an occasional question to get some clarity. She bounces her foot under the table. From your angle, her knee looks like a fishing bobber, peeking above and diving below the surface again.

The rest of your work history is rifled through. You skim and you dive. You joke, and you're sincere. Her words echo off the walls of the room and then suddenly stop, like a well-drilled orchestra. You string together sentences like chord sequences to keep up, hoping to match her precision and grace.

We'd make a great team, you reaffirm.

She nods some more, as if she can agree with your thoughts as they pop up into your head and seep into the space between you and her. But then her agreement seems to spread like a pasty balm for the cavernous, dull pain spreading around your stomach region. You ignore it.

There are standard questions about strengths and weaknesses. About qualifications. But your favorites are the ones about company culture. You sink your teeth in.

"As I'm sure you can tell, when you start to work here, you develop a certain attitude—*a way*, if you will—and that conduct will permeate the rest of your life. How do you take on and embrace values in and out of the workplace?"

No additional reading was necessary to prepare you for this one. Years of practice have you primed. As a kid, you would go around hugging, kissing, and striking up conversations with your parents' friends.

You did this, in large part, because your brother would never do such a thing. It wasn't coming from an authentic place but one of winning people over, of getting points. You weren't always proud of it, but you learned how to do it well. If you have become qualified for anything, it is this show. The act of doing what you're supposed to do and being rewarded for it. The real-life theatre production of being good, even if you didn't feel good about it.

And so you remember a quote you put up on social media when social media began. The quote was by J. D. Salinger, written in 1961.

> "I'm not afraid to compete. It's just the opposite. Don't you see that? I'm afraid I will compete—that's what scares me. That's why I quit the Theatre Department. Just because I'm so horribly conditioned to accept everybody else's values, and just because I like applause and people to rave about me, doesn't make it right. I'm ashamed of it. I'm sick of it. I'm sick of not having the courage to be an absolute nobody. I'm sick of myself and everybody else that wants to make some kind of a splash."
> –J. D. Salinger, *Franny and Zooey*

And you also gesture, using your hands to make your point. You twist your face to show the flexibility of all your features, of your personality. It's glorious. You swear you can see her eyes sparkle. You smile big and fire away, in refined speech, about being a team player.

It's on so thick that you hardly feel it anymore. The mask. It's there to paper over the cracks. It's there to do the thinking for you. A built-in autopilot. It's there to keep you aiming toward the destination—to get you what you want, however you might be feeling at any given time. Results. You don't know what's happening with that increasingly sharp pain down below, in your belly, but your mask is made of invisible Teflon. You could take bullets and blades to the torso, to the limbs even, but the mask would remain intact.

"Great!" she gasps when the whirlwind is over. "I'm relieved to hear you really *get* what we're about."

If you weren't already smiling so wide, you'd stretch it just a little further.

"Do you have any questions for me?"

"You know," you say. "I do."

You ask her about how she got to the position she's in. On the one hand, you're being genuine. You're really asking because you want to be in her place one day, doing the hiring and the selecting, and making the judgments. In fact, you kind of want to be in that exact chair, and hearing how she got there might help you make better decisions. The added benefit is that, by design, this makes her feel good. Bonus points. Cherries. Everyone loves to be admired, and nothing helps a mask glow brighter than illuminating the person it's facing.

"My career actually started in a strange way . . ."

You grunt approvals. You look into her eyes but, no. You aren't fully listening to what she has to say. It's not that you don't want to. You absolutely wish you *could be* comfortable enough, be relaxed enough to step into her shoes and out of your own for a minute, but there's just no way. You're entirely too drenched in the swampy stress of the interview, and this only becomes more obvious the more you try to listen.

Can she tell I'm not listening to her? Does she even want me to? What do real professionals do with their personal stories? What are you supposed to do?

You decide that it's okay that you can't listen to her. When all the feel-good stuff is peeled away, this is ultimately a transaction; the rest is scenery. She just wants to know you're going to make her life easier and not harder. You're here to show that you're the path of least resistance. To be an avatar of the good employee.

Her retelling of her journey pours out into a broader conversation about the nature of work itself. It's here in this gap about work with a capital *W* that you make a show of letting your guard down. The power of positive thinking is foremost in your mind as you dish on experiences with pure energy, your travels and trips to festivals. These are exaggerated, of course. Some of them have even been borrowed, so you keep the details vague. The truth is that your life up to now hasn't had room for much beyond what you'd call *basic diversions*. And so you're in the bind now of having to show a more complete package of yourself when the very things that would have made you more well-rounded were things you sacrificed to get here in the first place. Deviating too far from the path would be dangerous. It would only widen, not shorten, the distance between you and the room where you want to one day find yourself. Rooms like this one, with people like her in them.

The two of you jive about music. You revel in the artists you love, and you go a bit overboard about loving the artists she loves. The conversation smacks with "heavenly" and "spiritual experience" language. You prop these statues up to stand as evidence that you're also the kind of employee who knows how to have a good time *and* can "go there" when the time calls for it, even if it requires some fictionalization.

"To be honest, I had to take a sacred pause from festivals lately," you say in summary, breathing lightly before what you suddenly realize could be your interview mic-drop. "Because they exhausted me—distracted me. I knew I was destined to work at a place like this."

She laughs in a way that says, *I totally understand,* and whether she does or doesn't, you're ready for this to end on a good note.

"Before we wrap up," she says, sliding the resume gently away from view. "Will you tell me a story?"

Your face tightens. Jaw clenches.

"A story?"

Your shoulders harden like boulders. This wasn't part of the script.

"Yes. Tell me one story where you—just by being you—felt proud of being yourself."

The knots in your gut are now dangling like gruesome ornaments on your exterior as if you are a Christmas tree in the late stages of deconstruction. Your imaginary parents shield their eyes.

"Well . . ." You pause.

You've been turned inside out. Completely. Your insides as now as wide as a canyon. The dam bursts. What were tidepools of uncertainty grow into tidal waves of doubt powered by those ominous thirteen words—you've counted them.

"One story where you—just by being you—felt proud of being yourself."

These waves crash and splash into the void. Automatically, the sirens blare. A billion of your most qualified mental custodians rush down to siphon the water back into the reservoir, to reinforce the walls of the dam. To get things under control.

Proud of yourself? It's hard to think of anything with that feeling or tone. How can you be proud if you've spent your entire life to this point hiding? Your ability to conceal, to cloak—maybe there's a source of pride there, but even in that chamber, there's the knowledge that it's all false. It's a structure built from the smiles and nods and stamps of approval. You glance quickly over at the bench where you imagined your parents earlier.

"Focus, honey," your mom says confidently. "You are destined to answer this correctly and get the job. Your brother did it. Your father did it. And you will do it as well. And that is why I am proud of you. Because you are living proof of our destiny. Keep going. You will do it."

"You know what you need to do, and I am proud of you for that," your dad adds.

You are the latest in a line of family members to go down this path. To take this oath of greatness on the path of success. You know that by doing so, you will be loved and you will survive. You don't want to die.

And the idea of being given love for doing the right thing seems like that drink of water you've been thirsting for. You must answer this correctly as they all have before you; otherwise, you will be burned down in a faraway village and covered in your ancestral ashes. You must survive at all costs.

Don't rock the boat. Give her what she wants to hear and live to see another day. This is how you all survived.

You glance over again at the empty couch where your parents had cheered, cursed, and coached you. It's empty. You're not sure where they have gone, but this is not the time for questioning. The stakes are too high. It's time to fall in line.

You open your mouth.

Be a good employee now and tell her what she wants to hear.

What follows is the strangest collection of words you've ever assembled. You grab pieces of reality. You glue them to slabs of invention. You stumble upon makeshift details and throw them into the pot. Your eyes drag themselves across the room like they are a spatula, sweeping anything and everything into the mixture.

You find yourself talking about this very instant. This very interview. You contort yourself and hold shaky poses, the whole operation always a feather's tickle away from collapse.

"So," you conclude, trying your best to maintain eye contact now that the carnival ride has stopped. "That's my roundabout way of saying that here, at this very moment, I'm proud of being honest with you about myself and what I can bring to the team here."

It's as if you've been stripped naked, save for the one part of your body where her attention seems to rest. The mask remains. Your face betrays none of the difficulty your mind and body are enduring. Over the years, you've perfected the art of playing it cool. If nothing else, you know how to look the part. The world could be burning down, but you could smile. It's chill. You're chill.

She stares at you for so long after you're finished speaking that all you can think to do is hold your breath like you did when your parents used to drive through tunnels.

"You know, I remember what it was like being your age, at that crossroads, and trying so hard to choose correctly," she says at last. "I spent so much time and energy worrying about doing a good job. Do you ever worry about that kind of stuff?"

If her last question sent you scrambling, this one just sails over your head like a rocket headed for outer space. Now, you're just trying to get out of here in one piece. She must have things to get back to, right? Hopefully, you didn't make her feel like you needed help or someone to talk to—that would be the biggest disaster of all.

"Funny you should say that," you say, finding the perfect truth to share. "I'm actually the person so many of my friends go to when they're freaking out about work and existential crises. For advice."

She takes a long, deep breath, nodding her head.

Then, as if waking up from a dream, she stands. She thanks you for coming in. She says she will be in touch soon.

You think you orchestrate a clandestine rub of your sweaty palm against your pants under the table before shaking her hand goodbye. It's only after you've exited the office that you remember the table's surface was made of glass. You try to recall what was outside the windows, behind the spot where you imagined your parents.

An amusement park attraction of some kind?

But now it's all a blur.

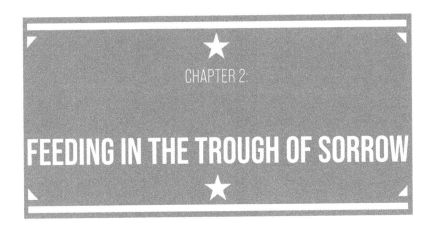

CHAPTER 2

FEEDING IN THE TROUGH OF SORROW

Y ou hadn't lied to her. You really are the one your friends turn to for guidance. When you were a student, they asked you about school assignments. Once you graduated, everyone wanted to know how you navigated your career path. You didn't worry much at all—you had your plan. Your parents were on board, and their approval outweighed your nagging desire to see and call out the nonsense pumping through and staining the whole social system. That plan, stains and all, became your identity. The smell didn't deter you from marching along, playing pretend. You just kept going, thinking if you went far enough in the system, you'd get past the stench. From neither the outside nor the inside, there wasn't much cause for stress because you'd never really failed at anything. But something has changed, and if you are being totally honest, you could have intuited it coming.

To prepare for the interview, you'd accepted a friend's gesture to stay—temporarily—on his couch. This was the friend who got your resumé to the top of the pile in the first place, through a contact of his. The position had opened quickly; they told you about it because you'd asked, and then you jumped. Both of you were confident you'd get the job. The stay on the couch was just a transition between the "now" and the "when you get hired" and finding a place of your own.

But now it's all been thrown into doubt. You only squeak out a couple of confirmation texts to your parents that your interview had indeed "gone well." You screened their probing calls.

There is still nothing to discuss. In the minutes and hours and days that follow the interview, it feels like all you can do is wait. It feels like an eternity passes. Then, you wait some more.

What else can I do?

In fact, you find plenty to do. Any distraction is a good one. You clean your little work area. Organize your files. Catch up on the world's latest breakdowns. Watch those shows. Listen to those albums. Read those words. Write your own. Paint.

Each distraction is better than the last. No matter what brand you choose on a given morning, afternoon, or evening, it's laced with your favorite flavor of neurosis. You don't believe in superstition, right? You just notice how often certain things seem to pop up.

Like that number.

Look no further than the number twelve. Twelve episodes in a season. Twelve songs in an album. Twelve words in a paragraph. There are even times when there are exactly twelve words in a sentence. Additionally, there are twelve-letter words. Stories posted on news sites at 12:12. Twelve loose items floating around your desktop: documents, spreadsheets, PDFs, videos, songs, apps, folders, photos, presentations, resumés, poems, trash. There always seem to be exactly twelve pieces of debris covering your little corner of the living room, both whenever the cap is on your water bottle and when it's not.

Am I looking for the twelves, or are they looking for me?

You start showering in a twelve-step process. That's how many paces it is from the bathroom to your bedside. You no longer find it weird that most drinks get finished in twelve sips. Dishes big and small, tasty and bland, all get cashed after twelve bites. Twelve is divinity. Twelve is what can't be ignored or over-exaggerated. Finding twelves assures you that you will be taken care of.

"Have you ever noticed twelves floating around?"

Your question hits your friend's face like a pie on a black-and-white comedy show.

"Dude," he says as you remember, this isn't the first time you've asked him this question this hour, the hour of 12:00—as in noon. "Chill."

But you don't. How could you? You push the chip towers into the middle of the table. This is all or nothing. You do or you don't have what it takes. You're in or out. Right or wrong. Good or bad. The split in the road is killing you. The longer the moving sidewalk you're standing on takes to get back to solid ground, the deeper the doubt.

Your friend means well. What else could he mean? You're living on his couch as this entire thing evolves. You can't imagine he wants you there long term. Having a guest is one thing, but being a guest is another. Neither of you can exist like this for much longer.

The two of you have been friends for years. From college. Or was it high school? Work? An internship? Mere proximity? A friend of a friend? No matter; it's not like the past is what glues you together, anyway. You're merely a pair who share the same ambition: to make the most out of life. To seize the day. To turn frowns upside down. To reframe all that negativity into positive thinking. *To make it.*

"I'm trying to chill," you say. "I'm trying so hard, but I'm just stressed."

You confide. You describe the specific stress the waiting causes, trying to be more articulate about the layers to it—yet again. You talk about how sandpapery your teeth taste. How they've been grinding against each other wildly since you exited the company building. You don't even know how bad it's gotten. Your friend tells you he hears the dental carpentry at night, all the way from his bedroom, but he figured it had been a neighbor doing a remodel. You think the stress is causing the headache you feel coming on, but you learn, it's actually your teeth.

"Or is it that I'm stressed because I'm trying so hard?" you ask.

"Just breathe—just take a big breath," your friend says when you've finished and your headache is good and pounding.

You count twelve breaths. The ins and the outs.

Is that twenty-four, then? What constitutes a full breath? The pair or just the in or the out separately?

"It will be fine," your friend continues. "Whether you get the job or not, you've got a place to stay here for a while as you figure things out. If you get it, awesome. If you don't, you're more than qualified to find another opening somewhere soon. You aren't going to starve. You aren't going to wind up on the streets. There is nothing to worry about."

Except there is—yourself. You have a full armada ready for nuclear war on your own sense of self-worth if you don't get this job. You had it all in your hands. No one else was there to ruin it for you. There are no excuses. That was the shot. That was the opportunity. Then again, you can't help but realize the irony of the payoff you'll receive if you failed: you'll be right. Everything that voice deep inside you has been saying all these years, that voice you know belongs to *you* and only you—not to your parents, not to your friends—will be confirmed. Not getting the job would validate and prove yourself right about how much you suck.

Teeth on teeth on teeth, like a DJ scratching needles against needles.

"Breathe," your friend says again.

You close your eyes and opt to go full nose for the breaths, doing six exhales and six inhales. As you do, you swear you can feel your heart pounding inside your brain. "1, 2, 3, 4, 5, 6, 7, 8, 9, 10, 11, 12." Your eyes shoot open.

"Why don't we go for a walk?" your friend suggests.

You wonder if that's a metaphor for you getting out of his house for good. A walk has some appeal, but inside, you feel an anvil weighing you down further into the living room, into the couch, into your phone. There is no way you're going for a walk at a time like this. A time like this calls for control. A time like this calls for you to honor the anvil that seems to pull your blood downward like a magnet to the floor. It's all a sign, you tell yourself, to keep you glued to your phone. You watch your attention race around this track of distraction and can't see where walking fits in. You let your friend down easy.

"Thanks, but I'm good for now."

And so you dive deep into that rectangular window—the one universe you tell yourself you still have control over. You like your friends' photos. You survey your exes' posts. You comment on random contests and repost them to be entered to win. You walk like a zombie into the kitchen, phone plugged into a backup power supply stuffed inside your sweatpants pocket, charging cable dangling out like an umbilical cord. The microwave clock says 12:12, and you're too hungry to care. You eat leftovers of a spicy noodle soup, then dive into a pint of ice cream with the same oily spoon. You scroll and your thumb hurts and your eyes are like dried-out raisins and you keep scrolling toward oblivion. With every tap and flick of the glass, you feel as if you're putting planets into alignment, shaping the universe to make it adhere to your taste. Sometimes this makes you feel so good that you almost forget about the job completely. Almost.

All along, the focus of your conscious being remains on the contents of your email inbox. All notifications are on full blast. You see every message as it arrives. Promotions from online stores come. Dispatches from friends come. Reminders for upcoming events. Life itself pokes through the cracks of the concrete slab of "read" emails, but you trim it every time. You're just looking for one incoming outcome, one email. You're here on your friend's couch, parrying life away in pursuit of that paradise, landing that gig. It's all collapsing in on itself, the scope narrowing into the tunnel that is the next email. That email. Screw everything else.

It arrives at lunchtime one day. Of course, you wouldn't even know it was time to eat if not for the notifications of Special, Limited Time Deals that fill the screen space on either side of the message, promising to wave delivery fees. Your finger hovers over the bold message long enough for you to read the preview:

"First of all, I want to thank you for your interest in the position. After reviewing candidates . . ."

Your heart races as if trying to escape the shadow of the anvil that's now been released and is plummeting its crushing weight down an infinite number of floors toward the solid earth that is your bones and internal organs. It's almost not worth opening, but now all you want is the pain. You want to feel the burn and the wrath. Times twelve.

Craaaaaaaaap.

Then out loud and longer and without counting, "Craaaaaaaaaaaaaaaaaaaaaaaaap."

Your pulse is now ratcheting up, pushing you into hyper drive, but then the world seems frozen in place. The paintings on your friend's walls all hang pitifully. You hate them. You think the place looks absurd. The furniture style is wonky, as is your friend's taste. The environment is suddenly toxic, and you've been sitting there stewing in it.

No. It's me that's toxic.

You've been polluting it. It's actually a great place. Beautiful. Those art pieces aren't shabby imitations; they are heartfelt accents to an upwardly mobile lifestyle. The furniture is modest and practical. It's you that's the problem.

No. No. No. No.

No. You don't get hired. Worse still, the language in the email is boilerplate. Same email sent out to dozens, dozens of dozens, hundreds of dozens of others, who also missed out. You barely catch a glimpse of the last sentence, the only part of the message that seems catered to your personal interview.

"I wanted to get something more personal from you," it says. "Next time, don't be so afraid of your truth."

My truth?

Your truth is that you fall. You fall while lying prone on the couch. You fall down several flights of emotional stairs, hit a skateboard, and fly into the street called Harsh Reality, where you get hit by a bus called Your Dismal Future, decorated with giant advertisements of all the places you will not go and all the things you will not have. Ever.

Your parents. The truth is your conversations were so foolish. Their encouragements, all for nothing. No fodder for them to brag to their friends about. You don't even want to talk to them. You don't want to see them. Even though they are still months away, you start thinking about the most reasonable excuse to avoid going home for the holidays.

Your career. That was supposed to be the path. Not this. This is nothing. This is bad. Wrong. Not what the books led you to believe would happen.

So stupid to think you were like her, a no-ceiling type.

You flush yourself down and plunge yourself back up for what seems like several lifetimes; all those solid pieces of earth you thought you had inside now disintegrate into dust. You don't even realize you haven't eaten all day until your friend comes home around sunset, and you reveal the big news as a burning spear pierces your guts.

"Here." He offers you half a sandwich from his leftover lunch.

You scarf through it as he talks about his day. You don't hear a word of it. You eat and you ruminate on the email, staring at a crack in your friend's floorboards, trying to calculate how you can tuck yourself into a narrow enough shape to squeeze down there.

"So," your friend says at last, looking down at the shattered shell you used to call your body. "How about that walk, then?"

You watch yourself go, even though you interpret his offer as him seeing your worthlessness and trying to save you from it. Good luck.

The air would feel fresh if it weren't so lifeless. It's not hot. Nor cold. There's no breeze at all. It's one of those days that's between seasons. Stale.

You scratch your arms as you walk. Your friend asks what's with the rash. You hadn't even realized, even as your fingernails got caked full of dry skin deposits, that your arms were all scaly. But of course, they are—they've probably been that way for days. It's all part of the darkness, the despair, the abyss. You knew it already; you've just been waiting for that last shove off the cliff.

"I know I'm being a bummer saying things like this," you start. "But now I can't imagine why they would have hired me to begin with."

You make sure your tone is so compliment-starved that your friend can't even honor you with a response. You proceed in silence, but the universe screams. It begs for your attention. You can only avoid looking up from the sidewalk for so long. When you give in, you are smacked by the billboard messages. Everything shouts, "Hey! You are definitely not on the right path." You take it personally.

Am I the wrong person?

Good thing your friend is accompanying you. You almost walk into traffic on several occasions. He talks. You do everything you can to listen, just like you did in the interview, but the inner debates win again. The scratching persists.

A curse? Plague? Is this abuse all punishment for not reading the signs right?

You're lost at sea, and you can't find the buoy of discernment to save your life. You're not in the position to look something in the eye and deviate from any old ways of being. Any step off the boat is just another chance to fall into the water, where a patrol of sharks secures the perimeter with sharp teeth.

You notice nothing but the billboards on the walk. You have no idea how long you're gone, and you're back before you know it. At home, you do as much nothing as you can. You dive into your phone. You sleep. You wake up and dive right back into your phone, starting it all over again.

That initial moment of denial is dark, but the next several days are darker. You do things you shouldn't. You eat worse. It's fast-food delivery. It's desserts for snacks. It's booze for breakfast. Controlled substances for lunch that remind you of your mediocrity.

You harm yourself in ways that only you know will inflict the maximal pain—an architect of your own epic demise. The misery spreads like a virus, encompassing other past embarrassments, especially in the arena of love. You dive deeper into the online lives of your exes, especially the ones who would never have worked out. You deride yourself for all your flaws. You reconfigure the stories of the past to make the misery of the present more logical. It's you that's the problem.

I don't even deserve to be in the room. No matter what I do, I am going to fail. Just when I think I'm getting ahead, I will be destroyed.

You pull hairs out of your face, from your entire body, one by one. You stop counting to twelve and shake your head when you think of your foolish superstitions. You rip away your fingernails and toenails— the former with your teeth. You use the longest of the nail shards as a barbarian floss sword. You never had anything in your teeth to begin with besides all the plaque buildup from skipping out on the last several dental visits. You don't even have a dentist. You bask in the grossness of your body as if to demonstrate the heights of your unworthiness.

I am ugly. Fat. Disgusting. No one will love me. This thing I call my body is just a repulsive shell.

You relive the interview in your imagination. You relive it in your dreams. You experience the same event dozens of times over the next several days, all the same trauma and fear that you had in waiting to find out if you got the gig. No rinse. Repeat. No rinse. Repeat. Today feels like yesterday, and that one felt like the day before. You exist in past tense. The fibers of now have all but vanished as you sit in that theater made for one, re-watching several renditions of the same horror show called *your life.*

In the long skid into the funhouse of personal horrors, your friend eventually convinces you to go for a second stroll. Blood oozing from potholes on your face where you've squeezed even the most minimal acne bumps, scalp sore from digging into it with your jagged claws, lips raw from gnawing on the edges, and looking at it all in the mirror, you decide, yeah, you should probably get the heck out of the house. You need a break from yourself.

Days have passed since your last walk. You're not sure how many. You never paid attention on the first go-around enough to recognize this was the same route you walked the day you didn't get the job. The exact same. This time, you notice things about it because you have nothing left to say, neither internally to your subconscious nor externally to another. Your friend doesn't know what to say either. The two of you have said enough. You have nearly stopped listening to him entirely. And you suspect he hasn't been listening to you. You're not even sure if you've been talking out loud. You guess it's been mostly in your head.

The sharp squeaks of birdsong and the warmth of the sun are the first things you notice. The little breeze, when it comes, is next. You can feel your blood pouring into each of your limbs like a scientist pours solutions into glass beakers in a lab.

On the edge of the neighborhood, where the houses give way to storefronts and restaurants, the two of you pass other people. You see a small dog. It yips in your direction. The owner shushes it.

Right before the retail area begins to give away again, back to a residential area, you pass an empty storefront. It has a rectangular sign taped to the door. It's not glowing. So you don't think about the words. All the same, you're drawn to the sign. It feels like it's calling out specifically to you, and you stop to read it. The top line is written in big bold letters:

Cap'ns Want'd!

You have to read it several times before you get that it's trying to say, "Captains Wanted." You already think it's the strangest sign you've ever seen, and that's before you read the description beneath.

**"Find yer job, ace yer interview,
live yer life 'fore da storm comin' ta kill us awl up!"**

"What *is* this?" you ask aloud.

Then it hits you. *This must be it*, you decide, laughing.

This is your "rock bottom," and it's made of molten lava. Your veins feel like hot coils. Your mind spits out a grab-a-number ticket stream of insults at the kinds of losers who would bite for such a horrendously written, obscure call for employment. You feel like punching through the glass door, grabbing the sign, and strangling it to death. Instead, you just stand there like a tree, a tree being eaten by the lava.

"Huh," is all your friend can utter as he looks over your shoulder at the sign.

"Huh?" you say. "Huh?!"

You turn around and start stomping away. Your friend scurries after you. "What?"

"Yeah, exactly. What kind of sign is that supposed to be, anyway?"

"Not sure, maybe somebody—"

"Maybe somebody didn't finish school? Maybe somebody needs to think before they write. Maybe—and I hope this is the case—somebody is just playing a joke."

Your friend stays silent after that. It's just the sound of your and his footsteps on concrete. Even the birds seem to have vanished.

"Besides, Captains Wanted?" you continue, barely realizing you're talking aloud. "Who believes they are already a captain? Are there just these wandering captains with the audacity to think they can pilot a ship right out of the gate?"

Your friend stays quiet. Your mind does not.

This is just for people who already believe they're the business. There aren't even any promises of the kind of work being offered. It's just a simple, get-rich-quick, visceral-level, click-bait-in-real-life pill, claiming it will solve some loser's problems.

The two of you get home, climb the stairs into the apartment, and barrel inside.

"It's like a God Saves promise." Now that you're talking out loud again, you're certain. "Too easy and egotistical and all-encompassing to ever be true."

You sit down on the couch that's become your safe place. You start scrolling on your phone, but all you can think about is the sign. You wish you had taken a picture of it so you could post it for the world to mock it with you.

The fixation deepens as the night wears on. You can't stop thinking about it. Worst of all, the more you think about it, the more there's something at its core that disturbs you.

You know, deep down, that you lack the courage to be an absolute nobody. Somewhere in your shattered dream state you still believe the world owes you a captaincy to call your own. You want to make a splash. That was why you wanted the job—it was a cannonball into the deep end. You wanted a splash everyone would see. The splash your parents would applaud from their place on the sidelines has wiped the water away from your fancy new swim goggles.

Wait. Was that job a ship to pilot, or was it just another leap off the plank and back in the water? Another diving board toward nothing?

It's true. It was just another chance to dive, not to drive. You know it, and it disgusts you. You want to be a proper captain all by yourself, and you hate that you saw your little dream pop up in such a pathetic state.

Suddenly, you realize you *are* crap.

Wait.

Your stomach rumbles.

Just have to . . .

You race to the bathroom and sit on the glossy throne. As you push, you inspect your surroundings. The kingdom you've failed to usurp spreads out before you in the form of your own flailing socks and underwear hanging in uneven droops on the shower curtain rod. Your toothbrush is a fallen soldier, laid down on its side, bristles kissing the black-hair-covered porcelain chasm between the faucet and the wall—you had just snipped your nose hairs earlier today, after all. Your toothpaste is smeared on the side of the mirror, a few stones suspended in blue lava.

You push harder. Your stomach hurts. Your breathing has all but stopped. You lean forward to double down.

The pain deepens. You try harder. Nothing.

Finally, when you feel like you're more likely to pass out than purge, you lean back. You close your eyes, drop your shoulders. And then . . .

Ptttttthhhhhhhp!

You laugh at yourself, unclench your body, and let go.

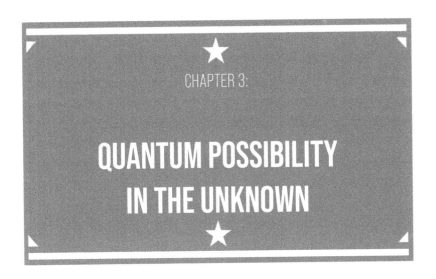

CHAPTER 3

QUANTUM POSSIBILITY IN THE UNKNOWN

n the dream, which you don't yet realize is a dream, you're back in the interview chair. Most of the room is the same—the plain art on the wall, just blurrier; the view from the window, just more vast. What's different is the chair across from you. Well, not the *chair* exactly. You never see that. What you see is a figure in the chair. It's not Ms. Xuan but someone else. You recognize the person yet can't place their name or from where you know them. The features on their face scramble over each other like reflections on the surface of a tide pool, and you're terrified to look directly at them.

The topic at hand, something you both seem to understand without having to discuss it, is the shame. You were young. You didn't know you couldn't do that. You didn't even really understand what it was you were doing. Beams of afternoon sunlight blasted through the guestroom window until you threw the heavy comforter over you. The peripeteia arrives, but you cannot—will not—reimagine it, not even in a dream. Back then, your personal self was a more foreign entity than it is now.

After the shameful event was over, your little, elementary mind tried to erase it. It's not like the lying started on purpose. It was automatic, the same as putting your hands out to protect yourself from a fall when you trip. These pleas for understanding seem to have happened somewhere on the dream timeline before you got here. Now, there is only this sense of shame about the shame and this hollow, sinking feeling.

Cold dirt covers your toes. The floor of the office has peeled away like tinfoil wrapping a candy bar. Underneath is a collection of raw, chunky earth.

Where'd my shoes go? My socks?

It's then you understand you've got no pants on—no clothes at all, in fact. The figure gently swerves back and forth in the rolling chair across from you with a blank face. No words are spoken aloud, yet it all gets worse. The sinking accelerates to become a pulverization.

Your ankles, shins, and legs are soon enveloped in warm, gooey soil. You open your mouth to talk, but nothing comes out. You want help but can't ask for it. Your chair vanishes, and by the time the dirt is up to your rib cage, you can feel the worms wiggling around in the moist dark piles that hug your body. You try confessing, even if it's only in thought bubbles.

I still don't know what exactly happened.

A headshake is all the figure in the chair can offer as you sink further down. Gravity works in slow motion. No words appear, but you can read the air.

It's only what I deserve.

Squishing your way into the ground, this sea of dirt swallows your arms, your neck. The figure bobs in the chair. The two of you are locked in silent combat.

What I deserve.

The flood of mushy earth crawls past your chin, your mouth, your nose. Its wet squeeze makes you wonder what kind of a pain death brings. Peaks of soil come into your vision, and you close your eyes.

When you wake up, it takes only a few seconds to realize you're still here. On your friend's couch. A wooly blanket discarded on the floor. Crisp morning air and rods of light cross through the open window near the bookshelf at the foot of the couch. Your legs are exposed. And your hand is down your pants.

Reaching for the water on the coffee table, your memory of the dream smears across your present thoughts like the condensation on the glass. The sparse details dissolve as soon as you try to hold them, like grains of liquid sand. Droplets of evaporating moisture.

Getting busy with your newly established morning routine of tidying up your little living corner and showering, your mind starts in on tasks of its own. You replay the interview once more. You struggle but can't remember what the interviewer said at all. You realize you weren't really listening. You can't recall even the most basic emotions or feelings emitting from the interviewer. *Why so few details?* You can't remember these about yourself, either. The whole thing feels like it happened in someone else's life, a scene from a movie you don't remember watching.

What could I have done differently? How could I have been more of a, well, to use that absurd word, captain? *Why aren't I there already? Maybe I am. Maybe I just had an off day. Or maybe the job really was just another roller coaster, disguising itself as home.*

You finish your shower. Afterward, the fibers of your borrowed towel brush against your slippery skin as you throw it over yourself like a cape. You've yet to wash it since you got here and decide it's time. Tomorrow. You shake it against your hair. Tomorrow will be laundry day at last.

It happens as you hang the towel back on its rack. You watch, almost in slow motion, as the weight of the saturated towel yanks a screw loose from the wall. A chunk of drywall pries off, leaving the whole apparatus slinking to the side. The towel, all slumped together now, is dangling just above the tile. First, you attempt to transform your fingers into screwdrivers. You press your finger pads into the *X* on the back of the screw and

37

turn. No dice. You stand back to check out the damage. The image is like a frowny face emoji in real life, but at least it's still intact. Then you ask yourself whether the rack was already like this before.

Yeah. You're almost sure it was. *Yeah, must have been.*

When you turn around and look at yourself in the mirror, you can't stare at your face for more than a few seconds before your eyes dart over to the sagging towel. The peeled scab of drywall.

You can tell your friend, but you know you can't fix it, even if you want to. Well, your friend has to have a real screwdriver someplace. Right? You had one in your old place. Didn't you? How do you even fix something like that? A bigger screw? What about the wall? How do you fix drywall? You don't have to get a whole new wall, do you? Isn't there some kind of frosting-like stuff that comes with an oversized butter knife? What about paint? How do you get the color right? Won't any new paint look weird against the old, faded color? Does this mean you have to paint the entire wall?

You leave the bathroom crime scene behind. At the pit of your stomach, rhythmic plucking vibrates bass strings. An echoing realization sounds through your body. Sure, there is lying and hiding and justification, but there's something else there. Then it hits you. You have no *real-world* skills.

Captain? You can't even fix a hole in a wall on land! How would you fare at sea? You don't know the first thing about sailing or navigation. You don't even know how to tie knots. There's a reason you opt to slip on rather than tie and retie your shoes.

You pull your head through your last clean T-shirt and start toward the front door. Walks have become the first rock in a new stack, the keystone of a pattern that emerges where chaos reigned the week before. Overall, these little citrus slices of routine are a needed spritz to the present slog. Never mind that it's already past noon. Time can wait. The point is, you feel activated. Little pulsating pieces of the body have lit up in your lower back and legs, adding an airiness to your movements.

The mere idea that the atoms inside of you have resonated with anything other than the stagnation of the previous period points to the hint of a shift occurring; though, at the same time, you also doubt it. You doubt it, but you still move forward.

"You can only take one step at a time," becomes the mantra your friend ascribes to, and it rings in your head whether he joins you on the walk or not. Today, he's gone already. Off to work at the office and engaging in important things.

You begin to slide your feet into your sneakers on the mat by the door before catching yourself. You untie them just to tie them back up. Proof. Okay, you know how to tie your shoes. But seriously—there is so very little else you know how to do in the real, 3D world. You've spent your life in front of a computer and wouldn't know the first thing about how to build the 2D things that pop up on it, much less how to create the screen itself.

Am I simply one-dimensional? Is that the problem here?

Whatever the problem is, you want to solve it, but you have no idea where to start; that's why you've been walking. Several days have passed since your big bathroom purge, and you still feel lighter. In fact, you feel so light, you're almost empty. Some days, you wonder if a strong enough wind could blow you off your feet, into the sky, and out beyond orbit. You could just float away. Solidity, weight, substance—that all seems to be at least part of the solution.

What's the rest?

As you continue this meandering search, there's one thing you can't seem to unsee. This "Cap'ns Want'd!" solicitation remains the most bizarre part of your days. The initial brush of anger it elicited has taken a more curious turn over time. In viewing the sign, you feel the claws of superstition ripping into your skin and wonder whether there will be any of you left if this keeps up. A person with no agency, a simple pinball ricocheting between literal and figurative signs.

But while the sign had seemed to come out of thin air, seeing it again and again on your daily walks activates your twelve-counting in more gnawing ways. You count the steps it takes you from when you first come into view of the sign's lettering until you pass it. Twelve, always, without fail. You even measure how your walks usually take about twelve minutes to complete. There are twelve characters—minus the space and the exclamation mark, in "Cap'ns Want'd." Rearranged to articulate what the sign is really trying to say, would spell "Captains Only." Exactly twelve letters.

What had been anger drifts into absurdity. Some days, you laugh at it because it gives you a chance to laugh at yourself. You blend trying and not trying, and it's a tightly wound narrative of how someone should act. This manifestation of life's silly incoherence. Sometimes the mere sight of the sign is a sweet surprise—a gift you may have never seen on a walk you may have never taken had things not unfolded quite this way.

Why does everything have to be so serious all the time?

You wish there was a way out. The absurdity is what gives in to curiosity that there might be a way out. Somehow, you just have to push through the dictator guarding the entryway, the one telling you what a piece of crap you are, the one repeating over and over again that your feelings are for the weak.

The more you consider the sign, the packing and unpacking of its meaning, the more it makes you uneasy. You try not to look directly at it when it comes into view, but as you pass, you read every letter, like an old typewriter hurling the inky keys pageward: "Cap'ns Want'd! Find yer job, ace yer interview, live yer life 'fore da storm comin' ta kill us awl up!" You can't help but autocorrect in your readings: "Captains Wanted! Find your job, ace your interview, live your life before the storm comes to kill us all!" and yet, you wish you had it in you to just let it go. You savor the way it pushes back against you, the permission it provides for you to investigate the incongruity within yourself. Then a bigger question emerges.

Where did I grow wrong?

The more time you spend considering the sign, the more a portal seems to open up around it. It expands, sometimes like a slowly widening flashlight beam, and sometimes so fast it's almost blinding. It shines a spotlight on what was the periphery of your perception.

Near the building, you've noticed a figure drifting. Their clothes are thick but tattered. A dank smell floats whenever you draw near. In a gap between the buildings, this individual has fashioned some collected things into a space of their own. A cardboard castle, a throne of old coats, pillows made from bundled plastic bags, a shopping cart steed— the whole package.

Is this a woman? Man? I can't tell. Were they always here? Who knows. Just keep going. Keep walking.

This expanding noticing spreads into something about these walks themselves. The way the emptiness allows for all this space where your footsteps echo. There is a battle taking place between the dictator in the mind and the awakening voice reflected in the sensations in your body. It's a new battle. Before, it was only the omnipotent force of negativity, and now, just for seconds at a time, you're allowing for some response. The feeble child of the body just wants a voice at the table.

But can I allow that? Maybe just for one second? We can go back to the old way of thinking; don't worry. But just for one second . . . can I allow that for one second?

The childlike voice pipes up, "No! Our feelings are deplorable, and they are weak, and we need to move on."

I can go back to the old way of thinking and listening to you, but for one second can we try something new? Maybe just for the sake of curiosity?

"Well, all right," the childlike voice says. "But soon, we are going to want concrete solutions, or we are burning this whole house down."

On that particularly hot afternoon following the towel rack incident, with the sun beating down hard enough to make you sweat, you proceed on your normal walk. As you move, you feel a burning behind your ears, close to where your skull meets your head. It's rage or it's passion or it's something else entirely. The reoccurring dream you've been having—the shame and the soil and your buried body and your mind. They are all competing. They each want to lead the way forward, even though no one sensation will clearly explain where it intends for you to go. For refuge, you wedge yourself into the shade of the building with the sign. You stand there for a moment, desperate for a cloud, for a break from the heat. But the blazing ball of fire is relentless. You catch the wafting dankness from the drifter, whose makeshift lodge is nearby. You consider how silly your reliance on this whole walking routine has become, how you've impregnated it with this misshapen meaning. You ruminate on how it hasn't been *that* helpful.

Or has it? Why do I do this at all?

You should just stay in and sit on the couch. There's no point in walking. The movement doesn't make a dent in the movement debt you've accumulated. You'll still be fat and worthless, so why even bother? These walks are stupid. They aren't for you; they are for someone else who is better and more motivated.

Shut up, jeez!

You abdicate to that oh-so-powerful voice inside and agree, here and now, to never retrace these steps.

When this commitment has been made, you decide to read the sign one last time. Except now, the sign is different. It says "Captain's Training! Commit to Your Own Journey, Never Lose Yourself Again, and Cultivate Discernment."

Wait. This has gotta be the heat. Right?

You lean closer to inspect it. It's taped on with the same recklessness, the corners are as peeled as usual. Even the handwriting is constructed with the same squiggly lines. The same color of ink. For nearly two weeks, the words on it have always been the same. Until now.

Why am I seeing something else today? Have I lost my mind?

You lean further toward the sign, this buoy you've circled on all these swims away from your couch island. A blinking beacon in this seemingly endless lost-at-sea experience of your own making.

What that . . .

You curse. You snap your neck back and forth. Only the drifter is in sight, dragging a newly salvaged wood pallet along the sidewalk. Even at your most neurotic, you know this isn't a simulation designed to fool you.

Conspiracy exists in neat packages, not in the humdrum of daily life.

You lean closer, eyes narrowed for clues. Your curiosity screams loud enough to be heard by passersby—if there were any. Your heart thumps. Blood pulses through your veins. The very idea of the sign starts to rearrange you. Perhaps it's been a wet rag for the heavily caked face paint of your mask. It may well be the one opening, pouring light into the shadow within you. The crack.

Maybe I've just been reading it wrong all along?

A tingly feeling races through your body, the way a limb floods with life after it's been woken from a nerve-compressed sleep. It's all you can sense as you shift your weight closer, the reflection of the drifter disappearing from view as the door tilts open.

You experience a breath-mint, commercial-grade gust of cool, refreshing air. It's heaven. The heat behind your ears recedes. The act of deciding itself disappears. Your agency is inaccessible. You're just a bug drawn to a crisp, cool light. You couldn't help it if you'd wanted to, and you don't want to. You step inside.

At first, the room inside matches what you had expected. The light is sparse. Most of the illumination comes from the far side, where several sets of uncovered bulb tubes hang overhead. A paint-splattered ladder rests against the wall near the door, with a few cans and brushes set beside it. It's empty in a way that you can't tell if someone just moved out or is starting to move in. It seems like a space meant for business, but for now, it's simply a space between the past and the future.

Maybe a refurbishment is underway.

A paper-thin layer of dust blankets the small collection of items strewn around the room: a table saw, some lumber, a long couch, and a plastic plant. The door folds close behind you, and you walk through this odd playground of debris, each footstep leaving a newly pressed imprint of your exploration. Boot prints in this quiet, snowy valley where only a faint electric hum vibrates through the air particles. It's a shred of evidence that comforts you. Given how the day has unfolded so far, you wonder whether you are still dreaming.

Within a few seconds, the frigidity of the room suspends the day's sweat on your skin. The beady trails on your arm are sprinkled, like everything else, with a delicate patina of dust. It's like you belong here. An item already. Fields of goosebumps rise across your limbs all the same. Each breath is like an icy mint drop against the surfaces of your mouth. The dread that's hung around you like a heavy necklace the last few days remains cool and lightens—a hard, jagged pendant turned into a featherweight jewel. You've avoided direct confrontation with it, fearing how spikiness it is to the touch, but given its transformation, you negotiate. You and this imagined-yet-real object remind each other what happened the last time dread visited. This time, your organs suffer no hydraulic spasms. They remain still in this new space, such a departure from recent responses to dread.

The hot skull pain behind your ears also begins to cool down. The acknowledgment itself is like setting a piping hot pie on a windowsill where the open window lets in the breeze.

So you keep moving. The prospect of getting discovered or attacked or reprimanded is a possibility that becomes as absurdly fictional as finding the love of your life somewhere in all this vast dust.

At the other end of the room, under the lights, is a desk. It's the only object, excluding your physical self, that doesn't seem to fit here. The dust-covered plastic plant and the couch have a certain permanence to them but not you, not the desk. Halfway across the space, you glance back at the entrance before approaching the desk any further. The papered windows no longer reflect light from outside. It looks dark.

How long have you been in here? What happened to the sun?

You check your phone, and it flashes two different times in quick succession. 2:19 and 9:12. You scrape the dust off to get a better look. Now the screen won't show a time at all. There's an error message.

Is this what happens to everyone who comes in here?

Thinking about other people reignites the pulsing behind your ears. Questions cascade down about who else has been in here, when was the last time someone walked around like this, whether that person is the same type of person you are, what kind of person you are, who any of you are who are supposed to be in a place like this. No answers come and that's about all you know for now, and now is all you have at the moment. No phone calls are waiting to be returned. You have no emails to reply to or reports to submit. No files to organize. Not now.

So you continue.

Up close, the desk is wide and sturdy. Confident. Built from ancient wood. Grains and knots float along in both curved and straight motions. Rounded edges give way to sharpened corners, blunted only at their tips by shiny bronze caps. Its legs spider out, cased in the same metal armor, and give the object a statuesque quality. You step across to get a view of the opposite side and find it's a mirror image of the front. No drawers or keyholes. No cabinets or knobs. Just a well-crafted dumbbell-shaped container with no way inside and sufficient leg space between to hold it up forever. All that's missing is the chair.

It's only then you realize the biggest oddity of all—not a single, visible grain of dust rests on the desk. It's a golden, hibernating beast in the silvery winter of the room.

Transfixed so wholly by the desk, you nearly miss what's on top of it. On the corner closest to the door rests a small, familiar object. It's a book.

Also free of dust, the cover is made of soft, faux fur. Picture a stuffed animal but in book form, a teddy bear but with pages. Instantly, you recognize it but can't remember how. What it jogs in your memory is a simple visit to the zoo when you were young. The buildup to seeing the savage magic of the natural world up close and in person, the letdown of finding the creatures caged, the tearful return home, the distance you started keeping from your childhood dog afterward. Now you remember. This book was a gift from your parents. A keepsake from that first zoo visit—the first book you remember.

It is your first story.

CHAPTER 4

BRAIN VERSUS HEART LEADERSHIP

T he last time you saw the book was on a trip to a used bookstore. It was long before you quit your old job—before you had the last interview on your radar. Years earlier now. In a low-lit corner of the store, the fuzzy spine had caught your attention. Fur can't exactly glow, but its fibers certainly shined. You brought the copy to the clerk with the spirit of a child on a treasure hunt who'd discovered gold where the X was marked. In the short conversation that followed, you learned your precious furry tome was mass-produced in its day.

"Everyone had one of these babies," the clerk told you. "They were like water."

This revelation cheapened the item. Suddenly, it felt flimsier in your hand. It was a gimmick, at best. A book dressed up as a stuffed animal to coax difficult kids into reading . . . seemed a lot of kids needed coaxing. You being one of them. Based on the cashier's reaction, you were the only part of the process that had been unique—in that you'd been uniquely duped. You had always thought the book was yours alone.

But the sharp teeth of the truth revealed that nothing was ever yours alone. Like so many others, you had siblings. Those siblings didn't just take and reclaim and destroy the physical objects you loved; they were also dragged into playing the game of the politics of family love and approval. Your parents spoke differently when they spoke about one child or another, it seemed. For some periods, you weren't a subject spoken about positively. At least that was the meaning you fabricated based on specific events. You perceived your grandparents did a better job of hiding it. Except they, too, couldn't escape survival mode. They encouraged certain behaviors through the push and pull of conditional love. Favoring one over the other was a way, you assume, to encourage physical survival but, ironically, simultaneously destroyed your ability to be yourself. Maybe that's why you clung to objects, like this book; maybe you had understood its pain.

Out of nowhere, you laugh to yourself. Maybe unconditional love is just a façade, anyway. Maybe there is some good in the push and pull of conditional love—a sense of honesty. A sense of joy and room to express that joy. What if no one owed you unconditional love, and it's just a made-up concept? You're alive and reasonably well. Isn't that enough?

Back then, though, the pain was dull but brutal. You thought you were special because of the rarity you assumed the item possessed. Following the experience, other objects of your affection—from movies to music to toys—revealed their ubiquity. Even their arrangement in your hierarchy of affection wasn't unique. The memories that made up your life, those things you told others you'd loved, had all been made in a factory. It felt as though you were on a conveyor belt yourself, inching along in some machine.

Much later, when the dream interview popped up, the excitement came mostly from the idea that the assembly line would add a new sparkly feature for you—rather than a shot at being removed from the standard-issue process.

That day at the bookstore, you grinned a big, fake grin—your best effort to be chummy in the wake of the letdown. Then you slumped your shoulders and escorted the book back to the section in which you found it. The copy's furry cover was warm by then, and before you put it back on the shelf, you flipped to page 79 and read. As you'd guessed, it made no sense.

How could it?

Your innocence was compromised. Your pulse had to match the pattern of the humming machine. To survive, your heart needed to harden.

Back in the present, inside this strange office space, you stare at the book a long time before picking it up. Its gray exterior is nearly the same hue as the copy you'd had as a child and the copy you found in the bookstore. Gray like a grandparent's hair but made of timeless, synthetic fur. Like fake flowers or plastic trees, a play at permanence in a world of constant change.

You flip through the book, ignoring the harder work of actual reading. It might as well be a tool to fan yourself with its "pagey" fronds. As chapters fly by, you hear a grumbly voice clear its throat. You look around the room and see nothing, no one. Then a red light flashes on the desk beside you. It's a button you hadn't noticed before. You press it. A small speaker rises from the desk.

"Salutations, *señor*," the voice says through the intercom. "Please forgive the look of the place. Know it's a bit of a mess . . ."

Your eyebrow perks as your fingers press into the faux fur on the book's cover.

"But see, that's why we're looking for would-be captains, to whip them into shape."

"What?" You put the book down.

"What do ya mean, *what?*"

"I mean, what's the deal? Who are you? Where are you? Where am I? What is all of this? Why would I want to be a captain?" You stop as you realize your voice sounds too harsh.

"Well, kid, truth is, yer already a captain. We all are. But who is at the helm? The head or the heart? The past or the future?"

You pause. The voice sounds raspy and raw. Suspicious. You decide it must belong to the author of the sign. Either way, you don't know how to answer the question, and you are too confused by the whole scenario to make any calculations.

"So which one, kid? Head or heart? Past or future?"

A tension crawls up your spine as you curl over to inspect the intercom. With your back bowed like a question mark, you open your mouth to speak, but nothing comes out. The muscles around your jaw harden. You're not tongue-tied like in the dream but tongue-frozen. Stoney.

"I'm thinking ya don't know how to answer the question, but something compels ya to understand."

Your usual masking process has been short-circuited. Without seeing the owner of the voice, you're lost about how to proceed. If this were a normal interview, with care given to eye contact and warm gestures, and not some rip in reality itself, you'd ask about what the position entails, what the responsibilities are, who you would report to, how you could benefit the organization—those sorts of things. Instead, you don't even know what questions to ask.

There are two captains inside? One in the head and one in the heart? What does that mean? Which one is better? I suspect living from or in the past isn't the right path forward, but how can I know the future? Why do I care, and, wait, if I could be hired for this "job," can anyone apply, or is some level of experience required?

In the delay, the voice speaks again.

"If ya worried about yer qualifications, have no fear. We got a training program for all new hires. It's free and straightforward, even if it is a little unconventional."

"Okay," you begin cautiously, like you're hearing your voice for the first time, "what's the application process—"

"Good news!" the voice crackles. "Yer application's been accepted."

"But I didn't—"

"Sure, no, I git it. In the extra fine, invisible print on the sign on the door it says, "By enterin' the premises, waltzin' over to the desk, and pickin' up the book, ya toss yer name in the sailor's cap to be drawn as the next captain."

"Wait, what do you mean invisible? And I only picked up the book because . . ."

"Ah, yes, the book. Thanks for remindin' me. Always forget about the book. Funny 'cause that's the most important part."

You've always been a fast learner—the most important of survival skills—so you know better than to speak mid-ramble. Instead, you stand up straight, uncurving your pinched spine, and wait for the next twist.

"But Imma gonna get to the book in a second. Lemme get some information 'bout ya first."

Despite all the reservations you have about this voice, this place, and the sign itself, a target appears in your mind. It's labeled *Redemption*. You have this sudden impulse to put the voice on the other end at ease. To boast about your qualifications, to gloss over a quick story of yourself, making yourself into something more than worthy. You want to one-up what you did in your failed interview. Instead, you want to show how overqualified you are for this position, to gracefully reject this open invitation because it is beneath you. Except you don't know where to start. There are no ledges to grab onto to scale this mountain. You don't know what to brag about. You don't know how to show qualifications for something you don't understand. You don't know how to frame the story. You're scrambling up a slick, solid slab of uncertainty, and as your brain revs but can't start its engine to follow a script, your mouth takes over.

"Me? Well, I am totally lost. I'm in an abandoned storefront somewhere and just crossed a desert of dust. For all I know, this is a dream.

So no, I don't know what I'm doing, and I'm not really qualified to do anything. I have no skills."

"Perfect," the voice says. "We love imperfection and uncertainty in candidates. Qualities like yers make the best capt'ins. Out there in the great expansive ocean, nature is so unpredictable. If ya know too much, ya won't react to each unique situation."

Right away, your body feels lighter than it has in years. Maybe ever. There is a feeling of truth, even honesty—a release that came with the admission. You are no closer to knowing what is about to happen, what the deal is with this room, who this voice belongs to, or what's next, but you feel way better. You know you're in the right place, kept afloat by that physical sensation.

Before you can respond, you are instructed to lift the intercom. Beneath it, you find a small paper with one simple message:

The book is the program. Don't forget. The program is the book.

"Ain't that funny?" the intercom continues. "I never 'member what's under the intercom, but I 'member there's somethin' there important to tell folks. I always 'member the book is important but never 'member to tell anyone about it."

"Wait, so I have these very specific memories with the boo—"

"So yeah, what was it that was under the intercom again?"

"It says—"

"Oh, that's right." The voice laughs. "Turn the back of the sticky note over."

You do as you're told. On the back is a small list of bullet points. The first one says,

- *A true captain must be able to reflect. Write a poem about cairns.*

"Complete the tasks and ya will be called in for an interview. After that, a job offer will come in no time. Always a demand for capt'ins."

"Okay, so what's a cairn?

"Wait. Ya don't know 'bout ducks, stonemen . . . come on . . . cairns?" The voice shifts its tone.

"Is it in the book?"

"The book? Guess ya could say it *is* the book. But that's our only copy, so ya better leave it there."

"Why don't I just take this one? These are super easy to find; you can just get another online."

"On what?"

"On the internet."

There is a long sigh on the other end of the intercom. In the interim, you grab the book.

"Look, fella, just put the book down or pick it up and git busy."

"But I know this book. I've read it a thousand times. What's the use in reading it again now? What's the use of any of this? Why bother becoming a captain at all?"

The intercom light turns off, and it winds closed. You pause for just a moment, then crack open the book. In it, you read the following again: "A true captain must be able to reflect. Write a poem about cairns." Then you keep reading.

ARCHERY/ARTERY

Younger days,
A time without a time, a memory, or fiction?
Youthful days playing games, eyes closed to the world.
Wake up! What use is the heart?
To confuse and disappoint?
To feel pain?
To feel controlling love?

To propel us or to incarcerate?
Is there something more, I ask?
Something outside these time zones?
Stuffed inside this furry page?
The stones stacked point out the direction.
Arrows straight from the heart.
There is something more, so take aim.

At the bottom: "Now your turn:"

You can't remember the last time you read a poem, much less wrote one. The thing about poetry is that it lives off ambiguity. There is no pressure for correctness. Just genuineness. There is nothing to protest over. Nothing to stop. Only pouring into space. Only floating.

A sharpened pencil rests where the book had been when you first approached the desk. Whether it had been obscured before and is now visible or it appeared from some secret compartment, or whether you conjured it up somewhere in your subconscious, none of the "hows" or "whys" now concern you.

Your body moves faster than your mind can tell it what to do. Actually, they are moving as one, neither leading the other, simply working as an undivided unit. You pick up the pencil. You sit down on the desk. You hold the book open with one hand and brandish the pencil with the other. You fill in the blank spaces with words of your own. Reflecting as effortlessly as a mirror. The lead scrapes the paper in an ancient rhythm that scratches an itch somewhere deep in your chest.

After your poem is complete and the space filled with words, you take the sticky note and cross off the first bullet point. You read the front side of the note once more:

The book is the program. Don't forget. The program is the book.

You place those words face down as a kind of bookmark between the pages of your poem and the example. Facing you are the other bullet points. The next one reads:

- *A captain is present. During your training, discontinue use of phones and the internet.*

At first, you scoff. You've sharply defined the filters for the behaviors that fit into *the kind of person you are* and those that don't. Having long since automated them, they reject this second instruction right away. You reach for your phone to take a photo of this hilarious suggestion to post online.

Wait.

You pat your pockets. You don't have your phone with you. The truth that dawns on you as you feel the emptiness of all your pockets is that some of the lightness you felt came from not having anything with you.

Maybe keeping the phone off for a few days won't be all bad.

Where a week ago that would have sounded like a recipe for boredom and distress, in this rawer state, you see the appeal. Your phone had been less of a communication tool and more of a bottomless pit of anxiety and depression since the interview, anyway. The training can't possibly take that long. No one needs to reach you so desperately that it can't wait a little while.

All at once, you experience an unclutching of your fingers. So often curled around the black rectangular screen, they straighten out, and your palms are allowed to stretch. The air around your entire hand feels refreshing, almost electric, yet still restful.

You decide it will probably be more exciting if you wait a few days before checking your phone. By then, you may have a whole bunch of messages rather than the one or two that trickle in throughout the day now. Presents to receive like greetings and wishes on your birthday.

You don't have to think about it anymore than that. You just need to go back and tell your friend what's going on. Still, this justification, while it pleases you, also feels like it is self-manipulation and fraudulent.

You close the book with your makeshift sticky-note bookmark, hold it and the pencil in one arm, and walk across the room much faster than you came across the dusty floor earlier. The light against the windows is bright again, and you don't even wonder what that means. You simply open the door and step back into the afternoon light.

The outside heat now feels cathartic after all that time in the chilly room. As your eyes adjust to the brightness, you notice the sidewalk beside the storefront has been broken open, not so carefully exposing the dirt beneath it. The cracked edges of the concrete have the appearance of unevenly snapped squares, like a chocolate bar. It makes you think of your dream, of the exposed floor in the interview room, of your sinking into the dirt. An echo of that hollow, sinking feeling creeps around your waist, and you have to remind yourself that you're standing on solid ground. Your fingers rub gently across the fur of the book cover as composite scenes from the shame flash like a camera shutter in your mind.

You circumvent the hole and stand gazing at the drifter's cardboard castle. For a moment, you admire the specificity of its construction and the way the new wooden pallet adds a drawbridge-like element. When it hinges open, you quickly resume walking and remain firmly focused on putting one foot in front of the other until you get back to your friend's apartment.

He isn't home when you arrive. It's kind of a relief. As good of friends as you are, having to talk through the whole experience in the room seems like a challenging task. Part of you knows he would think you've lost your mind, but the deeper issue is that you've had the first taste of mystery in as long as you can remember. Not having any idea where this strange bullet-pointed path will lead is exhilarating. It's something like the feeling you had as a kid when you thought about those fantasy stories your parents read you after your interest in stories was ignited by the fur-covered book. Explaining the experience logically, even to yourself, isn't working. Explaining it to someone else who wasn't there to witness it would be like . . . like puncturing a hot-air balloon just as it's getting full enough to fly. *Crazy.* Your friend might actually think you're nuts.

You leave your friend a note. You say you're simply taking a break from your phone and the internet for a while. You say the reason is to work on yourself and see if you can't find a way out of the hole you've put yourself in. That's a goal you know they will undoubtedly deem worth the minor inconveniences of short-term communication gaps.

Who knows, you laugh to yourself, *maybe I can afford to pitch in for rent with a captain's salary.*

Once the note is written and you've left it on the kitchen counter next to your powered-off cell phone, you crack the book back open. You look at the list, wanting to know what's next.

- *A navigator knows the wind carries with it valuable information about what's to come. Your first ceremony, Seeing the Seer, will show you how.*

That word, *ceremony,* opens up another whole labyrinth of doubts. Ceremonies have all these histories; history has all this baggage; baggage has all these rules, and that all sounds too heavy to drag wherever it is you're expected to go. Ceremonies sound like *shackles.*

You hear the word thrown around in those worlds you despise, worlds where people do the things they do to get the approval of everyone else. People use ceremonies to acquire things, lose things, get rewarded for things, or marry things. You hate them—the ceremonies and the people who hold ceremonies. You hate that part of yourself that hates them. Beneath that bristly feeling, though, you also know the skeptical part of you has something important to offer too.

What is the harm in allowing yourself to, just this once? Perhaps maybe, just maybe, there is something to learn here—or unlearn.

You set the book down, still cracked open wide at the spine.

Your next knee-jerk reaction is to grab your phone and search for the phrase "Seeing the Seer." As you reach for it, remembering that it's off, you realize how naked you feel without access to the information vacuum. Searching seems impossible without technology. The finding takes on a far scarier meaning when you've lost access to the map. In front of you, all you really have is the book, so you open it up and flip past your poem.

- *First Ceremony: Seeing the Seer*
  - Tonight at 8 p.m., just down the block, in the green house on the corner, with the blue light on outside the door, you will find the host, Marlene, waiting for you. After the ceremony, please flip the page.

The temptation to flip the page and find out what's to come on this weird training journey is strong. Too strong. But you want to honor the captain's tradition of respecting the process, so you convince yourself that you should not flip ahead, that you should be patient and take things one step at a time. That ruminating lasts, you guess, twelve seconds. Tops.

No one said anything about respecting any traditions. Captaincy sounds like the most tradition-devoid line of work in the world. Who cares if you flip ahead and see what's coming? Maybe that's part of it?

You've convinced yourself.

Funny thing is that when you flip the page, you find nothing. Well, not nothing. You find blank pages. You flip some more. IT's the same thing—more blank pages. Then, finally, a note:

"Congratulations. You've questioned the rules. Very captainy of you. But seriously. Get busy with your tasks. You've got a lot to do."

You flip through a few more pages, but they are all blank. You're suddenly finding it difficult to remember what the book you knew as a child had within its pages.

Well, I bet I could turn on my phone and figure it out . . .

No phone. No internet.

But what about just this once? Why would it matter?

But the no phones rule was written explicitly. You don't really need to know what your childhood book said at this moment. Do you?

Well, the voice also congratulated me on questioning the rules.

A neighborhood cat races by the kitchen window, chasing something you can't see.

"What part of the cat is in control of that instinct? The brain? The heart?" you ask out loud, to no one in particular.

And so you flip the page back to the matter at hand. Your first ceremony sits waiting, just a few hours from now and a few houses away. The green house. With the blue light. Seeing the Seer. Marlene—the host.

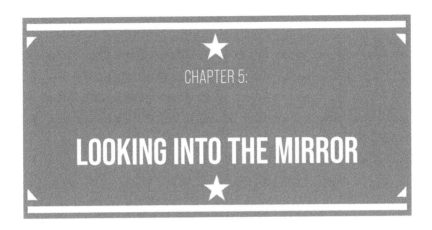

CHAPTER 5

LOOKING INTO THE MIRROR

Dusk has come and gone and night's darkness colors the path to your destination. You arrive at the green house on the corner. A bulb above the entrance soaks the ivy and wood gate in lazy neon blue. The skin against your face feels at once tight and elastic, like an extra-wide rubber band.

You ring the bell, and Marlene greets you.

"Welcome, brother," she says. "Follow me."

She leads you down a stone path around the main house, toward what looks like a converted garage. The two of you remove your shoes and step inside. Pillows, rugs, and a pair of low tables adorn a cozy space. Incense burns. Ambient music flows. Only candlelight illuminates the small room.

"Please sit, brother," Marlene says, motioning toward a cushion.

Bracelets and rings, woods and metals clamor together in a kind of traveling concert as she sits on a cushion facing yours. She wears spacious pants and a loose-fitting blouse with batik patterns. The lines on her face showcase a history that's neither young nor old. Softness is the central theme of her movements, her smile, and her speech.

"Is this your first time, brother?" she asks gently.

You nod, trying not to show how much being called "brother" bothers you, how it's yanking your skin more taught against not just your face, but your entire body. You know this is a test as much as a ceremony. You know this "training" is really a challenge to see what you're made of, and even if you don't know what the heck you're doing with this whole book-led adventure, you're here. You might as well keep going. You've got nothing else to do.

"Wonderful."

You can't tell if her grin means she wants you to start calling her "sister" or not. You don't feel comfortable enough for that sort of thing. You can accept watching the mystery unfold, but participating in it is another story, a bigger ask. This is a world you know only in clichés—through the quasi-spiritual equipment and New Age thinking that's dripped down into popular culture and memes in recent years. Some of it has even burrowed its way into the bite-sized business books you've gobbled up in recent years, but sitting here in the room with it now, your suspicion of it increases.

"Brother, tonight, we will explore a kind of alchemy together," Marlene says, with the backs of her wrists now resting on her knees. "It's been said the eyes cannot lie. That they are merely windows through which we witness the world unfolding. It's why we hear phrases like 'seeing is believing.' But would you believe me if I told you that seeing is only part of the experience of sight?"

You shrug your shoulders with your knees folded up like twin pyramids, your arms splayed back like kickstands.

"Would you trust me tonight, brother, to guide you in this alchemy? To lift the curtain for you to witness what is being witnessed? To see what is being seen?"

Shelving your reservations as best you can, you simply exhale and nod your head.

"Then let us close our eyes."

Stretched so tight, your skin feels liable to rip. There's something off about Marlene that you can't help but fixate on.

Or is there something off about me?

"Tonight, we will mesh traditions, ancient and new, wisdom inherited and learned, to fasten together a separate kind of sight. As brother and sister in this alchemy, we will transcend this realm and be transported into that deeper chasms of the ocean that are our lives. There, we will glimpse those waters we've never fathomed."

Her clothes, her words, even the composition of the room—in this dim light, these elements seem stitched together on a kind of patchwork improv. Marlene, the character, tip-toes across the stage of your tightened skin with her monologue.

A part of you recognizes these judgments are coming from a place of fear; you feel silly to have even shown up to watch the show because you're still uncertain about your commitment. Whether captains have to put up with situations where they question the captain-in-charge or whether this is some test on this strange journey is beside the point. The fact is, part of you is just watching yourself doing this, as if floating above the scene, and another part is doubting the whole affair.

"And in that space, may we both find healing."

You open your eyes without being prompted to examine her again, and she's beaten you to it. She gazes at you with the same softness that fills her words, and her hands graze your shins as she offers them to you.

"Give me your hands."

Her palms are warm but not hot. Touching them, you feel the coldness in your hands and fingers vanish. You feel a sensuality in the contact with her.

"Trust me, brother."

Now, instead of questioning her, you wonder whether she's into you. Sexual scenarios ambush your psyche. Pandora's box has been jacked open. And sailor-like thoughts ensue.

I wonder if she wants to get down. How hot would it be if we had some sort of passionate exchange in this little room?

Your hands sweat. At the same time, some cleavage poking out above her shirt becomes a memorizing sight, and it takes all your willpower not to lower your eyes. That must be another assessment of this unconventional eye exam.

"Look upon me with honest eyes as I look upon you and let us travel together."

Your throat is too dry to speak.

"Let's close our eyes and take three breaths, then I will reveal the instructions for this alchemy."

You close your eyes.

"Breathe in." She demonstrates with an inhale. She quietly exhales to speak. "For the next while, we will look into each other's eyes. Breathe out."

You use your breath to bracket the sexual thoughts racing in your mind.

"Inhale," she guides you. "This is not a staring contest. You can blink as much as you need to. Exhale."

Marlene is friendly and warm. It throws you off. It—she—can't be real. There's gotta be something else. Something she's hiding. You are skeptical of her, but you're more curious about why. How often are you already looking at the world with skeptical eyes? So what if she's a quack? Maybe there is something to learn, and just because she's hiding something doesn't make it all phony. If you always discarded the infant when you pulled the bath plug, you'd have sunk in the sewage a long time ago.

"Last breath." She draws air through her nose as you follow along. "Even if you lose concentration from my eyes, don't worry; just bring your attention back to them. Okay?"

Another nod. The two of you exhale the last breath in unison.

"Let us open our eyes, brother, and begin."

The first thing you think about as you stare at Marlene is something rather unexpected. You've yet to discuss any costs or payments with Marlene. They weren't things explained in the captain-seeking instructions. You've put away some savings. There are a few modest investments you can cash in if things get dire. You know, deep down, that you can return hat-in-hand to your old company, ask friends or family for favors, or simply string together some odd jobs, but this is the first moment when it hits you: You have no concrete idea when you'll be getting a paycheck again.

Money and sex? To be inside this quiet, dim room, embarking on this exploratory voyage for skills, and all I can think about is the bottom line or lust-filled fantasies? Is there something wrong with me?

You feel a dull pain in between your shoulder blades. It's like a screw is being driven into a hole half the size it needs to be to properly absorb it. The burrowing vibrations rattle against your spine like a didgeridoo.

It can't cost that much. Twenty minutes of staring? I'll be here an hour, tops. This isn't going to drain me of months of savings. I'll just leave a modest tip and move on to the next chapter.

Marlene stares back at you, and her gaze feels probing. It's like she's asking questions without speaking. Like she wants to enter the debate to say her piece.

Her voice enters your head. "What's so scary about money? Not having it? Having too much of it? What does enough look like? You're not going to starve, after all. Are you?"

Yes, but what if having it will make you fall in love with me to carry out my fantasies?

Marlene hears it and replies in your head, "Wow. How did that thought come in? Push it out. You wouldn't need the money for me to like you, and you aren't even sure that is what you want, anyway."

Sorry. That was embarrassing. Now this is awkward.

Being goal-oriented has helped answer these questions for you in the past. You didn't worry about money because the goals you set were in line with creating and increasing the numbers in your bank accounts. Each milestone was like a new checkpoint on a mountain climb toward a wealthy summit. A summit where you could give without receiving. A summit that would allow you to dictate the direction of your life. A little nugget to pursue, to distract you from your responsibility of loving and being loved unconditionally. A little gold at the end of a long journey to avoid being in charge of your own happiness.

But what's the goal of this? How do I clear this checkpoint? How do I release this survival-mode baggage when it carries so much weight?

Marlene's breathing is so slow, she's almost still. She blinks infrequently but otherwise doesn't move at all.

How much time has passed?

You know this feels awkward. The last thing you want to do is start over.

Gotta keep pushing through. Gotta make it to the next checkpoint.

You blink a few times to reset. This allows your focus to shift from the noise in your head to the still life in front of you. When you do, you notice the shapes. Triangles and squares. Curved and straight lines. Circles. A collection of different elements that make up the whole being in front of you. The face. Marlene's sketch. She blinks her eyes again, and you're drawn further into her.

What's she thinking right now?

She's probably done this a thousand times. She might have an entire routine, a library of learned lessons on what to think about and what to avoid during these sessions. Or it's possible she's just getting started, that any missteps are simply evidence that she's coming from a place of authenticity.

Maybe she has a mantra in her head she's repeating to stay focused. Maybe she's so good at this that her mind is a blank slate. Or maybe this is all a mask, like me in the interview? Maybe she's having thoughts about my authenticity or my sexual compatibility—or her bank account?

You wonder about her story. You fill in the details it would take for a person to pursue a vocation like this in her spare time. You imagine the sort of training she did or did not go through to develop the skill to guide people down these pathways.

Is this what she does full-time? Maybe she's a trust-fund kid? Or maybe she has a rich husband?

You resist the temptation to look down to see if any of her various jewelry assemblages include a wedding ring. You guess she's unconventional enough that a ring or no ring wouldn't matter.

Why am I creating a story around everyone I meet? How do I know Marlene wasn't born into a family of New Age healers? What if she came to learn this trade through a grandmaster at the far end of the world? Would that make it better? Maybe she worked her tail off, saved up, and started this because it's what she really believes in.

The nobility and authenticity of her craft eat up a few more piles of time that seem to widen further and further out. Whether the incense is still burning or the music is still playing, you almost can't tell anymore.

Please, Mind. Quiet down for a moment. Listen. Let's just listen, if that's okay with you.

You decide her story itself doesn't matter. You can wonder all you want, and it won't get you anywhere. The rest of the room has faded into a murky nothingness. Your focus has nowhere else to go but back to the candle-lit face in front of you.

Mom?

Out of nowhere, Marlene—who looks nothing like your mother—has assumed some alternate version of your mom. You feel your mom's energy. Her love and her judgment. It's as if you can hear her encouragement and her impatience without a single sound. The job you failed to get makes its presence known between you. She's disappointed, but you can't tell whether it's at you or at your inability to tell her about it so she can share the burden. She seems not just suspicious about this whimsical captain idea but embarrassed that you've humored it this far, like someone who got duped into buying an infomercial product. She thinks it's nonsense. Your mother has been "there" in a sense of being present, the way mothers have been designed to be, so she's "here" now, too, gazing back at you and then vanishing.

Is there something more here?

Marlene becomes a map you hunt for clues. You connect the dots between the sparse freckles on her face like you're trying to discover a star constellation in the sky. You try to count the seconds between her blinks, the number of pointy clumps her mascara has divided her eyelashes into.

Where is she hiding it?

You feel your skin loosen its grip on your bones, releasing the strings of the coin purse. It's like the cells in your body have eyes of their own, and they've turned their attention toward this group search. This collaborative effort allows them to stop pushing and pulling each other.

Maybe she's not hiding it all.

The rattling of your spine has stopped. The screws that were driving into you have been so gracefully reversed that you hardly notice their threads rewinding out of your shoulder blades. Your back feels more like a puddle than a piece of construction plywood.

Maybe it's just there to see.

This person called Marlene starts to go away. This thing she has called a face smears like it did on the figure in your dream. What remains are these two stained-glass windows with disappearing and reappearing curtains.

There.

Even in the low light—maybe because of the low light—there is so much color. Set in a deep porcelain cream, is a stunning, jagged amber. You admire it like the surface of a planet through a telescope. Liquid splashes on and off the glossy surface of these pairs of identical artworks, like a windshield wiper on a misty morning.

Wait.

One of her eyes has this jagged hole in its amber ring. They are not identical. In fact, each has its own weight in the color. Even their charcoal centers assume shapes of their own.

Minutes tick by, and they feel like hours. The time you spend staring at her eyes lasts lifetimes longer than all those thoughts and stories that preceded them. When you remember that this will have to end, it makes your heart ache. Her eyes have taken on an amount of sacred appreciation you are unfamiliar with as an adult. It's one part the admiration you'd reserved only for your favorite childhood toys and another part the intimacy you felt when your friends shared a secret.

It's while you're trying to pinpoint this sensation that you start to see something else in her eyes—no, beyond her eyes. It's an outline of a figure. The figure is sitting down, facing Marlene. A candle flickers behind them, to their side, illuminating the shape of their head, shoulders, and torso.

It's you.

You see yourself in her eyes. It's like a mirror but less fixed, a camera lens but less mechanical. There's an aliveness to the reflection that has so much energy, you feel your pursed lips pop open in awe. You've never seen yourself like this. Even with exes and lovers and your grandparents, you've always only seen them in their eyes. You've never seen you.

It hits you: This is what *seeing the seer* means.

Marlene must realize you've crossed that threshold too. Or perhaps, she's just now been looking long enough to see herself through you as well. Maybe it takes time for everyone to get there, for the waves to calm down long enough to see below the surface. Maybe it's always this way. Different each time but always the same.

You ache in your heart for Marlene and for yourself. You ache for what it's like to be a person. How it's at once so hard to see yourself and others and yet so easy. You're embarrassed at how the money, the survival, the assumptions about her, and the fleeting sexual impulses all interfered and robbed you of this time spent seeing. You forgive yourself for passing your own judgments about your journey through your mother. You let go.

And without warning, the equipment behind your eyes roars to life. Warm water pools at the foot of your vision. A drop tumbles over the edge of your eyelid and slides down your cheek. Marlene's masterpieces are also wet. You can still see the outline of yourself in them, and in a way, it feels like you're the one doing her crying and she is the one doing yours.

"Thank you, brother," Marlene says, signaling that your twenty minutes have ended.

You apologize and wipe away your tears, but she shakes her head and grabs your wrist.

"No place for sorrys here, only gratitude."

Reality races back to you. You take in the room again, remembering how you came here, how you sat down, the whole reason for being here.

"How'd I do?" you ask, knowing it's not the right question but feeling the awkwardness of the circumstances gnawing at you. "Did I pass?"

The way she smiles reminds you that you're still unsure whether coming here was even a good idea. One thing is for sure; it feels way too late to stop now.

Thoughts return as she guides you with her words.

"I am grateful for your heart, your joy, for having the courage to live in your truth," she says, bowing her head slightly.

You're not sure how this works, so you simply add, "Me too." You pause, trying to sound more sincere. "I mean, I'm grateful for yours too."

Marlene asks you to lie down. She informs you this is where she will mesh the cultures of the various traditions that have "spoken their wisdom" to her. You do your best to have a clear mind.

"And please," she adds, "keep your eyes closed. They need to rest after all their work while your other senses come to their aid. This will help seal and complete their healing and ensure your ability to see past the surface will become a skill to call upon and strengthen."

Marlene begins by grazing what feels like a feather against your eyelids. She mutters whispered words that sound more babbling brook than actual language. Using the feather, she brushes your arms, legs, and stomach as if wiping away unwanted dust.

For an instant afterward, your mind dashes into a dark place. You hear the sound of heavy objects being moved around on the other side of the room. Suddenly, you get paranoid about whether Marlene is going to kill you.

I'm only in this room because of a sign I saw on an empty storefront; how do I know this isn't a trap? What if the whole staring thing is just her serial killer trademark? I even left my cell phone behind voluntarily—the one thing that could have rescued me!

Your eyes shoot open as you stare at the ceiling. You tilt your neck down and see her walking back toward you with a long object. You sit up and brace for impact.

"What is that?" You do everything you can not to scream the accusatory question.

"Made from termite-hollowed-out eucalyptus, the way it's been done for tens of thousands of years. This is a traditional Australian didgeridoo," she says. "Now, lie down, close your eyes, and let the sound wash over you, brother."

You lie back down and try not to laugh at your own nonsense. *Didgeridoo!*

The thick, whiney vibrations fill the room. She has to stop a couple of times and restart. You breathe and, with each breath, step away from the edge of your paranoia. After a few minutes of the digeridoo, Marlene makes an announcement.

"The next instrument is the *huēhuētl*, an Aztec drum that was covered with the skin of ocelots in ancient times. Let its rhythm sync with your heart space as you ready yourself to reenter the world."

She bangs the drum. You notice she's offbeat. You guess the percussion element is a new addition. You zone out as she stops playing and her feet pitter-patter toward the other end of the room again. You consider telling her, when this is all over, that the music portion of the experience leaves some room for improvement. As you compile the script of what you will reveal and how delicately to go about it, a round, heavy object is placed on your stomach.

"They say the singing bowl originated during the Shang Dynasty in China out of a measuring cup." She whacks the bowl with an object she drags around its edge, creating a sharp, elongated humming noise. "I say, the measure of any human is how they treat their body and what they feed it."

The pulsating metal of the bowl stirs your guts. It's surprisingly soothing, a massage for your digestive system. As the piercing sound fades out, you realize how hungry you've become.

"With your eyes still closed for a moment longer, open your mouth, brother," Marlene commands, rubbing a wet finger on your forehead. "There is one final piece of healing."

You smell the bright tang of citrus.

"Did you just put orange juice on my forehead?"

"Open your mouth, brother."

"Sister . . ." You have to stop yourself from laughing. "Are you going to pour orange juice in my mouth?"

"This is pure and natural aromatherapeutic food-grade essential oil," Marlene says. "A few drops on the tongue will help you keep the taste of this experience with you when you go."

More objections pop up in your head.

Is it potent enough to burn my taste buds? If you were to hide a little roofie inside a ceremony, what better way than in a seemingly innocuous essential oil droplet? Why trust her? Then again, why trust this book at all? Why trust myself?

Your stomach rumbles.

Oh well, at least it's almost over.

You open your mouth, and Marlene squirts a couple drops of orange oil on your tongue.

On the walk toward the door, you ask her a lot of questions about her approach, about where she learned her trade, and about how she decides what to blend together. You want to suggest rethinking the music portion, but you don't have it in you. You're not really listening to her; you're just asking questions to pass the awkward moments on the walk back to the entrance.

"How do I pay you exactly?" you ask at last.

"Brother," she begins, "it's I who should be asking you that."

"What do you mean?"

"In your eyes, I saw a shapeshifter," she says. "I saw you become a woman. I saw your race change. Your age increase and decrease. It was constantly changing."

"I saw yours change as well," you begin. "You were—"

"I'm sorry," she interrupts. "You must not understand me. I've looked into hundreds of people's eyes, and this has never happened before."

You stand back and look into her eyes once more.

Is this what she tells everyone?

The oddness of the end of the ceremony fades away, and you're back to considering how you must look now under the blue light, by the ivy, leaving the green house.

"I am grateful to have had you here," she says, slightly bowing. "Good luck in your quest to become a captain."

With that, she closes her eyes and closes the door.

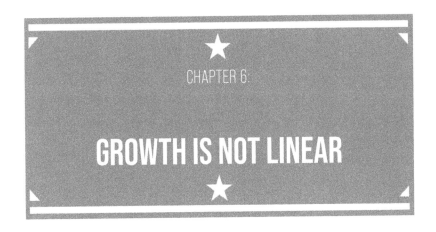

CHAPTER 6:

GROWTH IS NOT LINEAR

You've seen the seer. You made it through Marlene's ceremony without letting your judgments get the better of you. After an experience like that, you decide there is only one thing to do: eat a crap ton of pizza and chicken wings.

You walk to the local pizzeria, go inside, and examine the menu. The cashier makes fun of you when you start listing your desired items. She shakes her head when you order anchovies.

Uh oh. Is that a no-no here?

"What's wrong with anchovies?" a man in a trucker hat asks the cashier from behind you.

The cashier laughs. She's just giving you a hard time. She rings you up and while you wait for your food, you get to know Jim, the man in the trucker hat. He's fifty-two years old. He tells you he spends his days taking care of his mother, so when she's snoozing—on nights like tonight—he steps out of the house for a breath of fresh air. Immediately, you see the massive gap between your present experiences.

The seeing of seers and see-ees hasn't stopped.

Here you are, marching into the great unknown depths of your soul and your reservations about a world where victory seems murky at best, and for this guy, winning the day is helping his mom successfully use the bathroom.

"Listen, I used to be a chef," he says when you express that being a caretaker must be hard. "But I didn't like the competitive nature of it. I just want to make people happy with my food. The gift of having people say, 'Wow,' when they got surprised with a dish. I loved that. No ulterior motives. Just making good food."

You notice the way he goes back and forth between present and past tense like he might still go and be a chef again someday but is protecting himself in case it's not in the cards. Out of nowhere, he brings up his high school football career as a defensive end.

"Back then," he says, "I played light and fast even though I was some fifty pounds heavier than I am now."

He tells you his coaches would get angry at him because he only cared about the practices. He loved to practice, but when game time came, he relaxed. "In a way," he says, "I relaxed too much."

You decide there's something excellent about his relaxation that you can see, even now, and something beautiful in his role as a caretaker. It's something you envy.

"Maybe I'll just start waiting tables," he says as the two of you watch the cashier deliver some pies to a table nearby. Jim's eyes light up in a way that makes his words sound like he's making a commitment to sail around the world.

You feel a jolt of energy, like the experience with Marlene, which gave you the confidence of being on a new path. Even though being a captain probably amounts to the same sort of labor as waiting tables, you feel a sudden and uncomfortable pang of superiority that your path and pursuit are somehow more righteous than Jim's. You know it's false, but you feel this assumed hierarchy all the same. The judgment that followed you into the interview room, that you used to bludgeon yourself with, and that you brought into your experience with Marlene, is here too, with this interaction with Jim.

Suddenly, tasting that little leftover citrus singe your tongue makes you feel a little sick.

"If you didn't have to make any money," you ask, "would you still want to work?"

"You bet!" He laughs. "I think I'd still wait tables."

You marvel at the clarity. There's a simplicity and beauty in him that your judgments don't leave room for in yourself. In fact, there's been a straightforwardness about the entire pizza place—that anchovies sparked this whole conversation and the logistics around eating—but you've still managed to color it with your reservations and doubts. The world is showing you how it's right to the point. You're the one adding the frills.

"What about you? What's your story?" the trucker-hat guy asks you.

You watch yourself as you tell him about your evening in a way that's deliberately vague. Your awareness of your judgment turns in on itself, and now you don't want to be judged by this salt-of-the-earth guy who seems to have nothing to hide from you or the world. You start by calling the experience at Marlene's "a work training event," which your new boss "made you" attend.

"How was it?"

You just tell him there was a smooth take-off, a bumpy landing, and not much in between. It all sounds more dismissive than you wanted it to, but when the mask calls the shots, sincerity and truth have a hard time shining through.

"The last time I was on a plane," he says, seemingly out of nowhere, "the captain came on the mic and told us the ride was going to get bumpy. Then, like five minutes later, he comes on again to tell us it will get even bumpier than he'd anticipated. . . . I know, I know, some captain, right? But the thing is, I don't remember if it ever got bumpy or not. I dosed off."

Your food arrives. You hadn't realized it came with a drink. You've told yourself to stay away from soda, but here's a fat, two-liter for you to deal with. You grab the container of wings and the pizza and stuff them into a plastic bag you peel from the metal rod on the counter bag. Jim opens the door for you, and you offer him the soda as a parting gift, imagining how much of a good person it will make you seem and how you can safely get the poison off your hands.

"No thanks, brother," he says as if echoing Marlene. "I don't drink soda."

From the doorway, you turn and shout toward the cashier, asking if you can have unsweetened tea instead. She's on the phone and puts up two fingers in the air. You assume it means you need to fork over another two dollars. Immediately, your brain goes into defensive mode. You're ready to show her, just as you have with colleagues at work at jobs in the past, how her logic is flawed, how you deserve to cut through the unnecessary red tape and secure the unsweetened soda alternative. There's a touch of scarcity mindset in there too. Even though the ceremony with Marlene didn't cost you a dime, you find yourself on guard about money, knowing your pile is dwindling. As you mount your psychic warfare, she just laughs at you again.

"No," she says. "You can take two of the smaller teas instead."

She runs out, phone still in hand, and swaps the drinks for you. Jim watches the entire exchange. You can see yourself through his eyes, any goodwill you had built up for yourself now dissolving. The tables have turned. It's he who must realize how much more righteous his station is than yours.

"All that trying to look good," you say to yourself as the door closes to the pizza spot, "and it backfired."

You look back to see Jim turn his attention back to the cashier. *Now it's like I wasn't even there at all.*

The electricity, which registers as a manic energy that runs through your body and mind in the wake of the experience with Marlene, continues to surge after you get home and dig into the food. You replay the interactions at the pizza spot with more emphasis than you put on the ceremony itself. You reprimand yourself for judging Jim, for your desperation for his approval, for not being more honest with him about the experiences with Marlene, and for the skirmish that was never a skirmish over the stupid soda. You automatically grab your phone, eager to dive into a world away from your self-policing but realize it's off.

No phone.

You remember the silly rule. You remember the wonky book. The ceremony that you were so unsure about. And the bizarre sign that led to it all. All at once you remember seeing the outline of your body in Marlene's eyes.

What would she have thought if she'd seen me at the pizza spot?

You see yourself seeing what you did. You see yourself seeing yourself seeing what you did. Your behavior is not any less embarrassing, but for the first time, you're noticing it. You stop chewing the bite of pizza in your mouth. You see yourself stop chewing. You feel the savory dough nestled between your teeth. You imagine you're sitting across from yourself, watching yourself stop mid-bite. You taste the salty anchovy and wonder how it swam before being killed. You wonder whether it could see itself swimming.

It's the first time in your life seeing things this way. Sure, you've felt guilty before. You know compassion. You'd like to think you've had empathy when others suffered and that you can share in their joy. You just had never really seen your own self from any kind of alternate reality.

Curvy branches of a tree wave at you through the window, as if reminding you that whatever you are unlearning has already been unlearned. Beside the tree, there is a boulder. Both have evolved over time, surviving and existing just by being, and they speak to you.

"You think you are so clever, but all these realizations are actually reflections that exist in us from way before you were here as you are now. Look at me. Just being and living."

You giggle to yourself, and from there, the rest of your meal is playful. You see yourself eating a few too many wings. You know you are going a little overboard, but it's okay. You have a period where you see yourself as a good friend of yourself, enjoying a bit of binge eating in a way that's not dangerous or pathological.

It's okay. Everything's okay.

Later, as you're relaxing on the couch that's become your bed with your friend out for the night, you let your mind wander a bit, staring off into nothingness. You see how you were in the interview, through Miss Xuan's eyes. You see how you were through the eyes of your former bosses. Your old colleagues. Your professors.

How did I present myself to all these people? Why? What did I want them to see?

Then you think about how you appeared to those you've never seen but still needed—wanted—to influence. You think about the admissions board that reviewed your college application. Your essay was exaggeratory, borderline fiction, but it got you into a great school. Your reputation spread among your friends that you were the one who would present themselves to these faceless admissions boards.

Slinking back further into the cushions on the couch after recalling that admissions essay, you think back to today's conversation with the caretaker-trucker.

Have you always edited yourself for the approval of others?

In some ways, yes, and it has served you. It got you and others into great schools. You knew how to play the game. But it also left you feeling empty, undeserving, and worse.

Like a sham.

But even though this is a new realization from the mind-space, you recognize the feeling of the sham. In your bones, in your heart. The pain in the stomach as it pertains to a lie you were crafting or leading. Maybe there was something . . . someone inside, someone who knew all along.

Could that voice be yearning to come out to play, to be heard in the room? And then you also wonder what the part of you that needed to hide needed. All these parts of you—are you going crazy? Or is the craziness in not listening to what they each have to say?

Maybe learning it isn't so linear. Maybe some of it is buried in your past, but you're starting to pay more attention. Maybe it was remembering the embodied feeling you once had when you won that art competition, not because you wanted to win but because you wanted to paint for the sake of painting. And you begin to draw not only on newfound knowledge but the knowledge you've always had within.

Do captains paint? And if so, what hue are the colors they use? And does it all have to be so serious? Maybe the best captains paint things that remind them of what falls out from the crow's nest. Splat!

You smirk, and as you do, a wise skepticism creeps in as you reflect on how true—or fictional—your telling of your life story has been so far. You tell yourself so many stories about yourself and others, even about your friend. You want to determine whether this self-reflection is useful or not. You wonder if it's even possible to look at your life objectively. To look at the stories and their meaning, created separately from the actual events. You created those stories. Your best shot at safety is to arrange an entire armada of positively skewed narratives about yourself, ready to sail into battle against the fleet of automated negative self-talk. This all fuses into a lump of skepticism in your gut. Your tummy rumbles, and you consider whether you ate something foul.

The wings and pizza add an immediate impact on your stomach as you consider all of this. You take a trip to the bathroom. You stare at a photo on the wall of a rock cairn against a backdrop of mossy grass. You guess it's from Ireland or Scotland or some other faraway green land. It's always been there, but this is the first time you really look at it. You see yourself looking at it and put yourself into the story of its creation, listening intently.

You imagine yourself in miniature and place yourself on a mountain where you make a home inside this man-made structure of rocks. Perhaps it's of indigenous origin or was made by aliens. It's a little hill of rocks stacked like a pyramid, one on top of another, with one master stone sticking up from it like a sword atop this mini hill. You worship the main stone and focus on the big stones surrounding it at the top, paying no attention to the strength of the stones at the bottom.

All those rocks. Eroding and enduring all that erosion over time to become all of those sizes and shapes. Not having to give any effort to find their place in the landscape, simply being part of it.

Your breathing is the only metronome that brings you back to the present. You watch yourself judge yourself for the sudden urge to destroy the cairn. Then you catch yourself and decide it's ridiculous to want anything but to build upon it. Deep down, you know the wind and nature will have the ultimate say—not anything you do.

Remember when I arranged the stones to support one another, but then the wind came and knocked one out? At the end of the day what I was building doesn't stand the test of time. Entropy will force the rocks to tumble down, and the building of the structure will be a mere blip in nature's grand search for balance; my efforts will be in vain.

Still, you want to contribute to it. You want to add to it. You want to give back because it provided a home for you. So you shake the master stone, notice the location of its weakness, and do the same with the large stones. And it hits you. You can support the master stone with the smaller rocks. You can fill the crevices with them. These smaller rocks have a purpose. They are playing an important role in this art piece, in the existence of this masterpiece. Sure the big rock is important, but so are the smaller ones.

You can't help but consider the relationship between success and ego and how that parallels this structure, how you often think of the big rocks first, the ones that stand out, but in the end, it's all important. Your friend's work matters. Jim, the chef-turned-trucker-turned-caretaker, his work matters. Marlene's work matters.

Does my work, even when I'm not working, matter?

Memories of being young and having stomach problems pop up. Little lessons passed to you from your grandmother. An appreciation for your hands and body and holding, peeling, and eating an orange, to soothe your stomach after it was upset. The feeling of a spiritual presence in the citrus and its healing properties. That lingering taste of orange oil leftover from Marlene's ceremony. There it is, again, your breath, catching you and bringing you back to the here and now.

I have a sneaky feeling that maybe I do have some skills after all; they've just been hidden beneath the mask and the stories.

As you oscillate between your meaning-making and physically exiting the bathroom to walk back toward your couch-bed, you decide to look at the next item on the list in the book—because however many skills you have or don't have, you know they aren't immediately accessible. You bracket the lingering questions about yourself, your path, and your work. You hold that space suspended in your soul, instead of trying to decide one way or another, as you swing open the book's furry cover.

CHAPTER 7

SMELLING "THE TRUTH"

The road up the mountain sharply twists and turns. Jagged rocks stick out toward your car on one side as the city spreads wide on the other. Every few turns, there is a little half-circle of dirt that serves as a mini parking lot for those who have stopped to take in the view. Couples seek romance; motorcyclists break from their hairpin turns; families pop open their tailgates to break bread together. There's a whole assortment of people and activities and reasons. As the distance from civilization lengthens, the more you wind up the mountain, the more you wonder whether any of these paused observers are bound for where you're headed.

Perhaps they've been there before or maybe they will go there next time.

Before setting out for this mid-afternoon adventure, you took a moment to re-read the passage about the second ceremony in your *Captains Wanted* book. Every time you pick it up, without fail, a sense of doubt arises as your fingers brush the fur. Your torso feels like a hollowed-out tree trunk. It echoes when you ask yourself questions. The truth is, you don't know why you're doing this. In fact, you can't believe you're still doing it!

Am I delusional?

Maybe. And yet, here you are, along for the ride.

At least, you tell yourself, *it will be a good story.*

And so you re-read the book's next instruction.

• *For all the time spent in the slippery sea, a captain must value solid earth. Your second ceremony, I Smell Land, will show you how.*

Of course, you questioned going at all. Smelling Land has as much of a fishy smell to it as anything you've encountered so far on this strange, meandering journey. Plus, this second ceremony isn't simply down the block like Marlene's house. It is several hours away by freeway, up a mountain road, deep into a national forest. After sleeping on it, you decided the idea tickled your insides enough to want to know more, to want to peek around the next turn, to get up early, get in your car, head out to the woods, and drive to the peak.

As the groves thicken, you roll down your window. The air is sharper. Chilled. When it comes into your nose, it has a cooling, almost calcifying effect on the tumultuous energy inside you. Afternoon won't be around much longer, and the golden hour sends its beams of light like glowing spears, shooting through the trees, slicing the highway into two uneven paths. You can't remember the last time you went into nature on a whim. Your outdoor plans, like those you make with friends for dinner or drinks, for birthdays and bachelor parties, are bound by reason and time.

For you, arriving at a natural space, whether a mountain or a beach, a desert or a snowy field, means arriving there with goals. A checklist. With an activity to be completed, a social obligation to meet. Sweat or fun to be milked from the minutes and hours spent. Rewards to be reaped. In those games of hide-and-seek, trees like these disappear. The grains of sand flatten. The waves crash together. The snow tumbles into a void. Not since you were young do you remember looking out at these crews and legions and armies of trees and nodding your reverence, as you do now, sliding your way through them in pursuit of a small campsite beacon you'd broken your no-internet rule to map out.

You didn't know you were coming to the forest twenty-four hours ago. You haven't a clue what will happen to you, much less a solid objective to dangle for yourself at the end of the road now. No carrot on a string. You just have this beacon—blinking on your cell phone's map, which you aren't completely sure you shouldn't be using at this point— and the fuzzy assortment of earth stuff, cascading around you like crowds at a concert. And yet, there's this protective, heavy effect of being in the woods, something that lowers the temperature of your body, lowers your heart rate, and dims the lights of your hypersensitivities.

You veer off the highway and onto a dirt road. You're only on it briefly before arriving at the parking lot identified by your beacon on the phone screen. Curiously, several other vehicles sit idle and empty as you nestle yours into a space. Some cars are nicer and newer, while others are more rugged and seasoned. You notice how instinctive it is to create stories about the cars' owners as you lock the doors to yours behind you, before turning back to leave your cell phone behind in the car. Your phone long ago lost service, anyway. You're too deep in the mountains for status updates or emergency calls. Both the upsides and downsides of this technology you are so beholden to are wiped away in a short drive. How absurd it feels to be in and out of things in this way. How odd and easy it is to pluck yourself outside. You're enjoying the nakedness of not having the heavy box in your pocket. Increasingly, you're enjoying the untethered feeling you've fostered toward just being. Even your fears are taking a back seat to the throttle of the adventure and the realness of nature because the things that cause fear in your normal, everyday life fade into the background relative to the aliveness (and "deathness") you're experiencing in nature. It makes your human city experience seem small.

And if someone is out here to attack me, it looks like they'll have their hands full battling these other people as well.

You can't help but chuckle at the thought that these other humans might be looking at you fearfully.

You feel like a renegade, an outlaw. Even your muscles are firmer and more capable as they pull your body's baggage along, that hollow, wooden uncertainty in your core seemingly so impenetrable as to be petrified.

You follow the short path past some wooden picnic tables and benches. There's something soothing about this outdoor furniture. Its placement a declaration that this, too, is a room for people to enjoy. You take them are little invitations to slow down and stay awhile. You wonder whether the wood they are made out of was taken from trees nearby, whether these trees have simply taken another form and now rest on the same soil where they slowly grew and stretched out and swayed. These thoughts neither disappoint nor impress you. They simply pass by, like friends did in college as they waved their hellos between classes.

A stream runs next to the path. It bubbles along, a watery pet out for a stroll with you. It washes away your continued thoughts that try to make sense of the cars at the entrance, about who belongs to them. Like freshly penned sentences on a paper below a pouring faucet, the stream dissolves all these hypotheticals, this guessing and searching. It simply flows, and you stop, stand near it, and watch. You can't help but grin, feeling in a strange way like another tree that belongs here for its own sake. A diagram comes to you as if from a textbook in a classroom.

Thoughts	Emotions	Automation Actions	Being
• What you "should" be thinking or feeling • Value judgments on the feelings • Mental chatter • Meaning made from events	• The bubbling up of atoms within us • The way the atoms collide, frenetic vs. calm, open vs. closed, off vs. on energetically, slow vs. fast, grounded vs. high	• What we do to keep us from connecting thoughts and emotions	

You fill out this diagram without thinking about it, in your mind's eye, giving yourself a map to get back to where you are now in this serenity. You tuck it into a pocket in your brain and continue on. You march down the path to where the stream splits. Ahead, you see a group of people, some in bright and fashionable clothing, others wearing pieces more muted and worn. All the garments are containers, and in those containers wait a dozen beings, like you, with their experiences and their opinions, and their flows and blockades, warfare, and peace. You greet them and they greet you, and you find a spot on a stump between a woman and a man whose names you've already forgotten because the ceremony is underway, and your tardiness has invaded the calm like an angry mob.

A gentleman sporting a shawl, a dusty fedora, and a graying beard speaks to a part of the group with his back to you. Smoke billows over his shoulder. He's got the aura of a true mountain man, someone who could survive out here on his own for months, years even. You notice several of the attendees sit cross-legged. You try to follow their lead before remembering that being in that position for a prolonged amount of time only put parts of your body to sleep. You have no idea how long you'll be here, and you decide it's best not to push it.

I shouldn't have meandered so slowly. I should never have stood by the stream. I should have driven with a little more urgency.

You sit with your back as straight as you can make it. As someone who's spent most of his adult life hunched over a keyboard, proper posture is not your strong suit. In fact, pains speak up along either side of your lower spine the more you try to fidget yourself into a straight posture. Your abdomen isn't strong enough right now to provide the kind of support you need. Your lower back throbs under the strain. You've drawn your shoulders back to open up your chest, but it feels like you've gone too far, like if you draw them even a millimeter further, your ribcage will crack open like an oyster and your guts will be exposed to anyone, or anything interested in fresh meat.

You draw in a few labored breaths, the adjustment in the altitude making itself known by the effort required to adjust your breathing to sound settled and calm. You glance over at the others, but no one else speaks. For a moment, you feel like an intruder of some kind, like you've permeated a bubble that was sealed before your arrival.

Or maybe they are all wearing masks too. Maybe this world of ceremonies, like the world of career-ladder scaling, is simply another stage with its own performances and masked characters. Maybe the drama of captains is the same.

Whatever their mask status, none of these attendees are doing much looking around. Some are older than you, some younger. Most of them fit easily into visual categories of race and gender; some use their hair and clothing to signal their tribes, and others aim for ambiguity. Some have their eyes closed, while others have their gaze on the smoke.

The man with the beard is turning your way.

"Greetings, my band of wayward travelers," the man says, his face a leathery brown. "As those of you who have journeyed with me before are already aware, my earthbound name is Adolf Atahualpa."

"And yes," says this man who looks like a shaman but has the voice and candor of an AM radio host, "I'm well aware that the World War evil vibes of my first name and the Incan reverence of my second leave the meaning of these man-made sounds and titles confusing in your mind after receiving them in your ears."

He laughs with a devilish smirk. "Also, isn't it funny?"

He pauses and takes a sudden but long inhale, holds it for a moment, and exhales. Several of the participants join him as he breathes. There is something so much blunter about him compared to Marlene, something almost comedic and obscene but also something powerful and honest. You find yourself less concerned here because of his authenticity than you'd been at your first ceremony—and more captivated by his charisma and curious about what brand of weirdness he subscribes to.

"Which is the whole point," he continues. "Because this world is full of contradictions and as your eyes and ears do the busywork of meaning-making, your nose remains undisturbed.

"Yes, the White Man took tobacco—the great purifier used both in ceremonies of its own and to cleanse the ceremonies of other plants and traditions—and he turned it into a pollutant rather than a cleanser." He holds the smoke in his mouth, and, like the leaf which he turns into powder and puts up his nose, he turns a medicine into a toxin. The power of the medicine is not in the inhaling. It's about purification, about grounding, about the earth, not some other realm.

"But, you see, so few of us have ever really been here—in this realm—so to truly come here now, at last, is a sort of otherworldly visit. To see these trees, these mountains, our animal and plant brothers, these streams . . ." He looks at you. "To be here is to be somewhere magical beyond our wildest dreams and fantasies. If only we could get here, instead of there. If only we can find our way back to ourselves from that story we've told ourselves about our minds and bodies."

Adolf lifts a long, narrow pipe from below his poncho-like shawl.

"In what the White Man called the New World, tobacco was used for centuries to heal and to seal an agreement, with others and with ourselves." He raises the pipe. "It guides us humans through that invisible gate the natural world offers, into the spiritual realm."

He adds sandpapery mulch into the pipe's bowl.

"Today, we will use *nicotiana rustica*, nearly ten times more potent than its more common cousin, *nicotiana tabacum*, which you find in the White Man's death sticks." Adolf lights a match and sets the substance aflame. "And our bridge will not be called a peace pipe or the French *calumet*; rather, our Sioux sisters and brothers of the North's preferred term, the *chanunpa*."

Lost in the barrage and personality of Adolf, you've barely had time to take in the reactions of the other participants. You're transfixed by this man and this experience and the strange flickers of orange and purple now floating from his smoking pipe.

Is that the sunset hidden in those embers?

The second the floating aroma hits your nose, you feel the earth harden beneath your shoes. A force—the opposite of the numbing you've felt those times you smoked a cigarette outside a bar to calm your nerves before approaching a love interest—takes over. It feels like a sort of thawing, of being unfrozen, of mobility and control.

"Please," he says, "don't worry about what you should or should not do. Close your eyes if you'd like. Cry out if it feels right. Follow my words if you know them by now. Mimic my movements or sit still and simply observe. Let's begin."

Adolf faces the mountains just behind you with one arm up, holding the pipe, and the other palm open as if to receive. He blows smoke and then speaks.

"To The Winds of the South," he says. "Great Serpent. Mother of the life-giving waters. Wrap your coils of light around me. Remind me of how to let go and shed old ways of being. Teach me to walk the way of beauty."

His demeanor has changed. His voice has lowered several octaves; his speech has slowed. He turns to face the path you came from, with the same arm raised and the other open. More smoke bellows from him.

"To The Winds of the West. Mother Jaguar, support me as I see my fears. Teach me how to transform my fears into love. Remind me how to live with impeccability. May I have no enemies in this lifetime or next."

Wireframed geometric shapes form at the confluence of the smoke and the amber mountainsides—pyramids and boxes, shook loose from any gridded confinements. Adolf turns again, away from you like when you'd arrived.

"To the Winds of the North. Royal Hummingbird, Ancient Ones. Teach me about your endurance and your great joy. Come to me in dreamtime. With honor, I greet you."

Adolf turns one last time.

"To the Winds of the East. Eagle or Condor. Great Visionary, remind me to lead from my pure heart. Teach me to soar to new places, to fly wing to wing with the Spirit."

The oranges and purples are now exploding with all the weight of ripened fruit. Adolf places one palm on the earth, lifting the pipe with the other and blowing more smoke.

"Mother Earth, Pachamama. I pray for your healing. Let me soften into your wisdom. May I take great care of you so that my children and my children's children may witness the beauty and abundance you offer me today."

A firm, warrior kind of strength and solidity bears down on the clearing. It is a definitively masculine energy, a protective force. Then a sharp relaxation. Adolf sets the pipe down and raises both arms to the sky.

"Father Sun, Grandmother Moon, to the Star nations. Great Spirit, you who are known by a thousand names. And you who are the unnamable One. Thank you for bringing me here at this time."

Your eyes have closed without your knowing. An ancestral deity of great power, of warrior energy, a calming presence is with you. It points down a path toward something warm and vibrant. The space around it is a peaceful black matte-ness, where the chatter has ceased.

You feel the presence of Adolf standing in front of you now, closer.

"Keep your eyes shut but open your hand," he speaks softly, almost a whisper, and you feel something arrive at your palm. He slowly hinges your fingers closed around it. "Now bring that to your nose and inhale."

Where the tobacco smoke had transported you in linear directions and you felt the energy of the natural world that surrounds you, the scent that hits you now launches you into an entirely different olfactory direction. An airy, floral bouquet comes at you first, followed by a heavy bottom of wet wood and dirt. You imagine a miniature garden planter dissolving in your palm. You inhale again and are met, abruptly, with a sudden concern for what others are doing. You flash open your eyes and see they are all engaging in their own hand-cupped smelling, Adolf too. Fear creeps in about whether you're smelling correctly, whether you're focused enough, or whether you have allergies or a slight cold prohibiting you from finding the right messages in the scent.

Are they even smelling the same thing I am?

You notice your mind is walking you backward on a reverse path back to the car—unwinding along the road, back down the mountain. You're somewhere else, and you can see yourself being somewhere else. You see the seer, and you see a pattern.

This pattern is stitched together by fear, and you confront it. You remember other versions of this confrontation. You feel emboldened that you're getting better at it, seeing the traps of looking at others to better retrofit your mask to suit the occasion. You know these same kinds of traps can be manifested in all the other ways you seek to soothe with substance, with physical experience, with what you've called, at times, love. In acknowledging that pattern, you're able to sit in the feeling of the truth of it without feeling bound to it.

Smelling the smeller.

You inhale and let the lovely nonattachment flow through you. Through the scent, it's as if your body and your mind are dancing together instead of apart. Your mind is leashed, unable to wiggle away and toward its fearful training exercises, and your full self vanishes like the dusk light, far deeper into the quickly approaching night. The fear flows and tumbles like a waterfall. Creatures of the Indigenous tribes—the jaguar, the moose, and the owl—pay visits. You see them seeing you and feel the rumblings in their stomachs and the wind against their bodies. They show you how these sensations are what it means to be alive. They speak without opening their mouths and transmit more information than a library of books does, with a single tilt of their head. These unspoken voices feel much purer than all those you'd obsessed over before. The voices of your parents, the newspapers, and the interwebs are all replaced with more of a magical expansive blanket that covers you in a way where the future and the past—memories and dreams—combine into the now.

When it's over, you open your eyes and your hand. In your palm, you find a small cairn-shaped deposit of unburned incense. It occurs to you that the smell inside your hand was never hot; it must not have been burning at all.

"In the old days, ships were navigated by way of the tobacco smell from the storehouses," Adolf says. "That's how you could tell the direction of the winds."

You stare at the ash stack for a long time. Either a thousand thoughts—or maybe zero thoughts—hurricane through your mind. When you look up at last, you realize none of the other attendees remain.

It's only you.

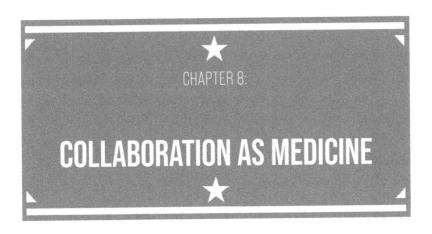

CHAPTER 8

COLLABORATION AS MEDICINE

Adolf, as if returning to another form, pats you on the back. His tone has changed, but his energy remains as thick and warm as leather.

"You ready to get out of here, bud?"

You join him on the walk back to the parking lot. The stream trickles beside you, sounding different in the cool evening air than it did at dusk. Thin light from the moon and the stars shrouds the trees you admired when you arrived in a kind of comforting secrecy. A safety. The earth itself feels firmer than before, and your feet grip it with more gusto, almost a suction. There's a dynamism to the hardened weight you felt in your abdomen when you came to the ceremony.

You and Adolf exchange basic pleasantries. You ask him about the relationship he has with tobacco, and he tells you how he came to it later in life and uses it daily to ground himself. When you ask him about the Captains Wanted program, he has no idea what you're talking about. When you ask about payment, he insists it's a free community experience.

As you wonder what any of this might mean, he tells you about his young daughter, who's probably causing her mother fits about her dinner right about now. With every new detail Adolf reveals about his life, splotches of color about his day-to-day existence emerge. You find yourself curious about what he does for a living but decide not to ask. Incomplete though it may be, you enjoy the part of the painting you've put together about his life and the mystery of not knowing the whole of it.

Back in the parking lot, you turn to Adolf. "Thank you," you tell him. "I feel great."

"I'm glad," he says, giving you a firm hug. "And remember that fusing healing traditions is complicated and should always be done with the utmost respect, so you ought to cut Marlene some slack."

"What?" you ask. "How did you—"

"Maybe there's a teaching and mentorship pathway that exists; maybe it's a quantum field of sorts," Adolf continues. "I'm not always great at articulating that which cannot be fully articulated."

The slightest breeze passes between you, and you let your questions drift away with it. "This might sound weird, but I just feel like you reawakened me to myself, to the witnessing of the seer, to the earthly," you say without really thinking through the words. "I feel confident, solid."

"That's great," he says. "But always know that movement is just around the corner. You know, changing states, solid to gas to liquid."

You cock one brow at him.

"The New Age folks don't always know how to break this down. I've heard it called 'spiritual bypassing'—a way you can use your experiences in a ceremony or some fancy terms you read in a book—to avoid facing unresolved crap that's piled up inside you over the years," he says. "They have an experience in ceremony and think they have reached some sort of pinnacle, like getting rid of their egos, just because they had this experience. The true warriors understand that a somatic experience is just the beginning of a larger process of integration in your body. It gives one a beginning, but it is not the end. The spiritual realm can't be used to bypass the hard work, not really."

You can't think of anything else to say or do, so you just blink.

Adolf looks right through you, adding, "Just because the cow patties have solidified into a cow pie doesn't mean it ain't stinking. And when you try picking it up, it'll just start smelling again, and you'll wish you'd left it alone. But you can't walk through trails all your life, hoping to dodge the cowpies with the nimbleness you've gained from some spiritual experiences. You can dodge them for a while, but eventually, they'll overtake the trail, and you'll fall harder than you did in the first place, into the crap. Unless you do the work to integrate the learnings into your body."

He claps his hands in front of your dumbfounded face. "Splat!"

You watch as he hops into his car, starts it up, and waves goodbye. Soon, the roar of his engine disintegrates into silence. Then your ears readjust to the easy ruckus of the nighttime forest. You lean against your car and inhale a few more plumes of chilled air, but the solid ground you feel is melting at the edges. No way around it. Adolf saw through you with his laser-beam eyes.

Being busy has been great. You've given yourself a pass to avoid thinking too much about certain things. Shame being chief among them. You know it's always there, the central cowpie on your path, but the prospect of moving it, even now, feels too difficult. It'd only stink up the place that is your present journey. After this period of feeling down on yourself, you'd rather savor these slices of newly found peace than try to kick up a ruckus.

Once you're back in your car, you reach for the ignition, but something holds you back. There's a smell in the vehicle you hadn't noticed before. It's familiar but distant, like a friend you haven't seen since your childhood. There is a sharp, wet citrus quality to the scent and a lingering sweetness that's soothing. For a moment, you sit with it, finding an unmistakable sense of home in it. If tobacco is transportive and forward, this is more a return to something you have no memory of ever *not* knowing. There's a flash feeling of the heat of the bright sun on your skin, of heavy, brutal summer humidity. You sense the scratchiness of your father's stubble and your grandfather's beard, the fascination with how, when you were young, hair grew on these men in your life as it did on the beasts in the wild. You inhale once more and see the wide grass fields and fountains in the parks of your childhood—places where your father and grandfather would bring you to gather with your friends and take the field, remade, as part of a team. It smells like the weekend before your weekends smelled like liquor and perfume and cologne. The scent carries with it the giving and receiving of being cared for.

You look around the car, trying to find the source of the fragrance. In the backseat, you spot a glass bottle you'd forgotten about. You don't remember how long it's been there. A day? A month? The cap had finally been shaken off and is on the floor, the few droplets of the liquid left inside, exposed. The winding road must have worked the bottle open, and with it, ten thousand memories from childhood escaped.

Agua de Florida.

All at once, you remember seeing a bottle of the cologne on Marlene's altar. You remember seeing it in your friend's house. You even, for a moment, wonder whether you saw it in the empty storefront where you found the book. Long before all of that, you saw the iconic, slim glass bottle of the cologne pop up at the gas stations and in the department stores of your youth. At your summertime soccer games, the mothers of the players would haul over a giant ice chest filled with water, ice, and splashes of Florida Water. Dozens of rags had been placed inside the cooler, sucking up the precious fluid mixture. At halftime, you'd dig in, grab the rag, and wipe your face with it. Then you'd leave it spread out over your neck and shoulders, relieving you from the sweltering heat.

In practical terms, it was meant to cool you down, but the full effect was something bordering on the mystical. Cooled by the ice and infused with the water, the cologne became so pungent as to become something else entirely. Both the bitterness of orange rind and the peak-sweet nectar of the fruit at its ripest combined with the blistering sourness of a freshly squeezed lemon delivered a physical sensation not unlike a set of defibrillator paddles placed firmly on your face, set on high. The surge was intense. The lingering floweriness that remained as you listened to your coach recount the team's strategy came from a touch of clove and lavender and something you could never quite place—a kind of new flavor that can only come when the right collection of other things is combined.

When your friend saw the bottle of cologne in your car when you'd first arrived in town after your move, he asked why you had it. You'd recently heard that Florida Water was used all over the Amazon rainforest in ceremonies of any number of spiritual traditions and places of worship. Ironic, you realize now, that Florida Water was originally developed as an allusion to the mythical Fountain of Youth, which, for thousands of years, was rumored to exist in different places, including Florida. Now, here it is, returning you to your youth, to those long hot days of passing, movement, attack, and defense—of trying to score.

All these memories come so easily. They require no thought. They are automatic. The scent works its wonders without your trying, even without your consciousness, barreling its way through your nostrils like a vapor massaging every cell in your body. This nostalgia floats into your chest, instigating a deep longing to return to those fields, to dunk your hand into the cold ice, and to pull out the pungent rag and rub it on your face. To be refreshed.

Ceremony.

Your mind flicks back on, and you discover that you're not as repulsed by the concept of ceremony as you once thought. You experienced it at every halftime. No one called it that, of course, but it was a *ceremony.* There was a process, a pathway, a departure from this world, and a return. A beginning and an end and a new beginning. A cycle of exhaustion and renewal, a washing away of the world of dust.

This realization feels electric. Where the tobacco had calmed and healed your anxiety and the interaction with Adolf about the cow pie on the trail had brought a sense of ominousness, this visit to your childhood brings with it a sense of playfulness. Of doing things for their own sake. Of fun. Of making instead of just taking. Of expressing something that's yours, the opposite of willpower in job applications and phoniness in interview settings. An opposite of normative success. It feels bizarre, but it also feels right.

But what does it mean? What do I do about it?

Above the Florida Water cap, up on the backseat, rests your copy of the gray, furry book, which led you up the mountain today. You look at it with fondness this time, a respect. It guided you through this vivid connection to the natural world, into this wonderful exchange with Adolf, and toward this brush with the spirit of your youth. You reach for it and open to the page that follows the "I Smell Land" ceremony.

- *You've Smelled Land. Now it's your turn to prove it to the rest of the crew without having to take them to the crow's nest yourself.*

You grab the bottle and fully inhale the scent now, closing your eyes and letting your mind drift back to those soccer fields. To what it felt like to play. To what it felt like to be observed. The pride that came with your parents and grandparents watching you in action, doing your best, sometimes winning, sometimes losing, but always trying, always pushing it.

You take one more deep breath and, before you have a chance to connect these thoughts to what kind of gibberish the book is sputtering out now, more memories of your youth float back. This time, there are others watching the soccer games.

Somewhere in those Florida Water-soaked days was the first time you remember trying to impress a girl. You can picture her now, brushing the hair from her eyes, whispering to her friend, the pair of them standing in uniforms of their own, ready to take the field when your game finished. This sharp awareness of a beautiful person staring, wondering, curious to know you.

Tina.

Of course, that's impossible. The young girl on the sidelines couldn't have been her—you didn't meet for another twenty years. But the way she stands, the way she watches, the fluttering feeling of having her attention—it's like she was always there.

You haven't spoken to your on-again-off-again ex in months, not since Tina moved to the desert. She left behind her corporate climb to pursue her passion as a perfumer, on her own spiritual journey to South America, the jungle, Ayahuasca.

More ceremony, more Agua de Florida.

Now you remember—it was she who first told you about seeing the Florida Water everywhere. It was she who inspired you to pick up an old bottle of the stuff before moving. You weren't sure why you did it then, but now it's clear.

It was ceremony.

Hunger strikes you now, with a force not unlike how it came following your experience with Marlene. That daily ceremony of breaking bread, with everyone from friends to strangers to lovers. No time spent eating sticks out as much as those spent with someone for whom you feel deeply. Memories of meals with Tina pour over you, mixing with the nostalgic vapor of your sporting youth, the growling of your guts, the flaring of your nostrils . . . all of this sits suspended over the four wheels below you, these four wheels that can take you anywhere you want to go.

From here, it all happens at once, as if in a sequence for which you flick only the first domino.

Both the containers separating the thoughts and the connections dissolve. The idea of scent itself eviscerates the categories. Stones skipping across the surface of a lake, these not-so-coincidental thoughts strike up a Morse code inside you. You flick the ignition and away you go toward the cactuses.

You're aware there are more pages left in the furry book to cover. You know this captain training plan is not over and this scent-capturing exercise is only part of a whole. Still, you feel driven by something else. Something deeper. Something that tells you it's okay to go off the path a bit, to take it way past what might normally be required. If being busy was to bypass and the job-seeking and career-achieving were ways to avoid, then this is a sacred, active pause to get somewhere else.

You're in a flow. You ignore the missed calls and messages on your phone when you fire it on. You use it to call Tina and talk to her over the several hours it takes to drive to the desert. Things were never bad in your relationship, and they aren't bad now. You ask her to pick a restaurant she likes and, ever the one for spontaneity, she agrees to meet you there. Once the time and place are settled, you click the phone back off. You decide the rules about captaincy are better looked at as guidelines, and you enjoy how you're playing with them, breaking and following the rules in your own way. It's fun.

Over a delicious Argentine dinner of grilled steak and salad, slow-cooked chorizo, and fresh chimichurri, you and Tina reconnect in a way that feels natural. You talk briefly and with levity about what you call a "career program," giving her some insight into the ceremonies with Marlene and Adolf. Letting someone you know in on at least some of the details of what's happening in your life feels refreshing, like showering after a long weekend of camping. Mostly, though, you find yourself asking about her.

"How does it feel to be living, more or less, off-the-grid, in the desert?

"Do you miss anything about the hustle and bustle of the 'real world'?

"What have you learned about yourself out here?"

Her answers are candid and complete.

"It's not all roses, palm trees, and hikes out here. It gets hot." She admits it also gets lonely. There are conveniences she can no longer afford, events she can no longer attend, and investments she can no longer plan for without the kind of salary she used to have. "And yet, there's a disappearing act I get to participate in every day when I work." She vanishes from time and place and the physical realities of her life and douses herself in the many fragrances she's composing as a perfumer.

"Since I was a girl, I've treasured smell more than anything, so I followed that urge toward perfume." You know her mother was a florist. Her father worked with leather, fashioning shoes, bags, and saddles by hand. In this way, there's been a return for her to a more rural, slow-paced life like the one from her youth.

The conversation meanders smoothly and gently, like a pleasant dream. A little residue of the actual words is left behind until she wraps and buttons it all up. As you chat, you find yourself touching your hands together. The scene is awash with feminine softness, almost as if your fingertips themselves feel like the inside of flower petals.

"I don't know that I'm completely *enjoying* it all, in the most vulgar sense of the word, but I'm thankful I get to experience all of life out here in the desert, in the same way a rock in the desert does—a watchful participant as it goes through life and life acts upon it, slowly but powerfully," Tina says. The actual eating of the meal has long since passed, and only a fraction of the Malbec bottle is left between you. "After all, I get to play scientist and artist at once. Every day, I get to toy with scents new and old and paint the air, in a way that's both as fleeting as wind and permanent as memory. I get to take someone somewhere without their having to open their eyes and see it, much less move."

Proof.

"I love that," you tell her. "And I wanted to see if you'd extend me an invite into your laboratory. I have an idea."

"Of course. I'd love to show you my organ," she says, referring to what she calls the *scent apparatus,* and by the time the two of you say your good-byes in front of the restaurant, you've agreed to meet the next morning.

Meanwhile, you find a small, refurbished airstream trailer to rent for the week. After the ceremony with Adolf in the mountains, you didn't so much as stop at your friend's place before heading out to the desert. Where the roughness of the mountains felt like what people call "masculine," the vastness of the desert feels open and what some might say "feminine." Despite not having a single spare change of clothes or much of anything else to prepare you for a stay in the desert, you feel great. Thrilled even. There's something so outlandish about what you're doing. The spontaneity is breathtaking. You can hardly sleep, you're so excited about it.

The next morning, you visit Tina's workspace. It is a cross between an apothecary, a nursery, a bar, and a chemistry lab. In a greenhouse-like atrium, she has several little workstations set up. At each, there are different natural materials being coaxed into powders, liquids, gels, soaps, and any other substance imaginable. She's only been in the desert for a few years, but it looks like she's been here for many lifetimes. She lets you smell some of her finished and in-progress creations. Bouquets of flowers, groves of different woods, and a jungle of herbs, spices, and flavors flow through your nostrils with the intensity of an unscrewed fire hydrant.

"How can you smell all this every day and not get overloaded?" you ask when you've sat down outside, where the wind acts as a cleanser for your nasal palette.

"Oh, I get overloaded every day," she says with a laugh. "That's part of the point."

You can't remember the last time you felt like this. Childhood? Those soccer days? Maybe you never have. You're all the way out here, without regard for time or goals. You just want to try something out and see what happens.

"So I want to create a scent," you tell Tina when she asks about your proposition. "I want to capture something I felt after the last ceremony I experienced and see if I can translate that into something that can be shared with others."

As a starter, you show her the bottle of Florida Water, and she laughs. She has a bottle of it too, a reminder of her trip to the jungle. It's a fragrance she's thought about using before but never actually played with. There's something about the citrus you both want to explore.

Over several days, Tina lets you tag along as she works, showing you how to use some of the extracts she has on hand. You encourage her to experiment with some items she's always wanted to use but didn't know how, or when, to try. There's something in the way she moves that reminds you of the wind—sometimes fast and deliberate, sometimes wandering and breezy. The tiny hairs on your forearms stand up as she whirls around you. Fresh air.

There's so much shared history for the two of you to dwell on and discuss. Memories of your time together flash through your mind, and you imagine she has her own moments of reminiscing. There's so much about the future the two of you could converse about too: how Tina plans to expand her artisan business, how you plan to use your new skills, what the two of you think about what's going on in the world, what it all means. Instead, you leave all the pasts and futures unsaid. You talk only about what's happening there: the way cedar bark and sandalwood share similarities and differences, how local and imported sage work differently with rose, and the way visible color and thickness can hide what the nose reveals. The rest of your time together is filled with silence. In that space, you discover a sort of deep smelling, whereby you deliberately listen to the scents instead of just hearing them. A wholehearted, nonjudgmental noticing.

In these periods of focused play, you consider what Tina described over dinner. You see how time and space themselves are upended. You realize that what Tina's doing in this ritual of her daily working is adding elements of ceremony into her routine vocation, which, a few years earlier, had only been a hobby.

You contribute to your new scent, but Tina does the most important step, the final mixing. You find yourself considering how grateful you are to be here, to have experienced the soil-like grounding in the mountains with a stranger, followed by this more floral swirl of energy in the desert with someone you know so intimately. As you marvel at this dance between masculine and feminine energy, Tina puts her hand on your shoulder.

"Thank you so much," she says. "I'd been feeling a little stuck in my work, plugged up with creative overload. Just the other day, I absent-mindedly clogged the sink. The perfect metaphor, no?"

Having her hand on your shoulder feels less romantic and fleeting but more bonding and true.

"You've brought a firmness, a clear direction, a purpose here along with you that I feel deeply," she continues. "You seem so alive right now. Your light is illuminating my entire space. I feel unstuck."

You're awestruck. You came to her seeking help. You hadn't considered that you could be a boost for her too.

She goes on to tell you it's inspiring to work with someone she knew in her old life and watch them find similar joys in this olfactory world. She tells you she thinks your scent is one of a kind, which even if it sounds salesy, you realize must also be true of all scents. The more she speaks, the more you see yourself through her eyes, your energy as reflected by hers. She means what she says. She seems magical. Just as you're having that thought, she reverses it.

"Thank you for your magic," she says.

I have brought something with me here. I've brought me, in a truer sense than I ever did when the two of us were together. I grew up with the shadow of darkness nearby. It was an upbringing where I was always coming from a place of lack, of needing something external to be acquired. But maybe I've been helping others too. Maybe I've been doing it all along.

It's only after she jots down the final ingredient list and you see twelve items on it that you realize there are two things that can't be gleaned from the order and amounts and temperature that comprise this recipe. Tina herself is an ingredient. As much as you are. You have a label made and are left with something to share with shipmates, so they don't need to climb to the crow's nest to smell the land for themselves.

When you are leaving Tina, she tells you she would like to give you the new concoction as a gift, but you insist on paying her in full. You tell her something you'd heard in passing, about how artists, especially female artists, can sometimes find it difficult to be compensated for their artistry, and you don't want to contribute to that dynamic. But she stops you in mid-explanation.

"Slow down. Breathe for a second. Breathe our scent together."

You do as she says. You breathe in the fragrance. All at once, you become aware that while what you were saying was true and intellectually sound, there was something else happening inside your body when she offered you the gift. You didn't know how to receive it. It made you uncomfortable. Maybe you felt you owed her something. How could you make it up to her if she gifted you something? And so you come clean to Tina.

"Listen. I wasn't being fully authentic there. It's true; I really do believe that artists like you need to be compensated, but I also said that because I struggle to accept gifts and love from others."

She nods, knowingly. "It would bring me great joy to gift my friend an expression of my heart. All I want in return is your presence and gratitude in this moment. In fact, I am thankful we're having this conversation because it means our relationship can deepen."

The truth of her words sinks in. Now you can talk about what your needs are, and she can do the same. She is sensitive to your discomfort around the acceptance of gifts. Her needs are considered even when you go to your place of fear.

Radical. Beautiful. Revolutionary.

Following the foray into creative scent-making with Tina, you decide to remain in the desert for a couple more days in the airstream accommodations. Instead of using the scent as an access point to access the memories of your youth—at the park with your father, on the sailboat with your grandfather—a new direction is charted. With the scent you made with Tina, you smell the hints of your creative abilities. Even before you'd finished constructing it, the scent became part of a new daily routine for you. You access that feeling of freedom through truth and honesty with yourself. What's soothing is the creation of self and not of fear. This routine hasn't arranged itself in anything as explicit as a ceremony. Nothing is etched in stone, but you have a feeling something is developing and momentum is building. Now that your feet are more firmly on the ground, it's easier for you to take flight and eventually land, even if the landing strip is a swamp.

CHAPTER 9

THE WARRIOR WITHIN

"I feel grounded but confused. Dark, stupid, not worthy. I feel scared. Yes, I feel scared. Scared and worried. Worried? I feel worried. I feel trapped. Unclear. I feel confused. And resigned. I feel kind of okay about it. I feel gentle. Joyful. I feel listened to. I feel kind of cheeky. Calm. I feel calm. Yeah, I feel calm."

These words are whispers. They come out of your mouth, meant for your ears alone. It's an exercise. It's helping you calm yourself down as you wait. Several other individuals are waiting inside the walls of a property. You've opted to stand outside, under an awning. There's a Joshua tree, several cacti, and some palm trees next to the sturdy walls of the cement compound-like structure.

The trick is to actually say the names of the feelings swirling in your body out loud, naming them like shapes of clouds passing by in the sky. Turning the vaporous feelings into words and letting those sounds crash against your ears is meant to show you how your body is merely a venue for changing vibrations. While all deserve their own time, none demand permanence when uttered so easily, softly, and routinely. Your voice lets them fly free. You watch how the emotions change quickly in your body. By doing that, you realize how your mind latches on to certain feelings rather than letting them move through you like ever-changing weather patterns that come and go.

As you realize how fleeting your emotions are, you think maybe it's possible to get less stuck to them.

You stayed in the desert because you wanted to sit in it, that creative feeling, that burst of inspiration, that realization that you, too, could help others on their discovery journeys. And yet, as the days ticked on, the grounded lightness you thought had become one with you took a different form. Maybe you misplaced it. It was like a jacket that you had on, took off, and then forgot where you had shed it.

At first, you played it cool, figuring it would turn up. For the first half-day, you tried to go about your business. You took a hike. You swam in a pool. You conversed with strangers at the grocery store. Trying to explain the grounded feeling and the tobacco ceremony in the mountains to others was hard enough, much less trying to link them to the impulse that prompted you to come to the desert in the first place . . . or the scent creation, or why you stayed.

Even with the freedom you found while talking to strangers—those who didn't know your old story or your bad habits or your better qualities from past experience—you felt a metallic resistance coating your throat from deep inside when you spoke. Your voice sounded like rusty aluminum when you spoke your tin, rattling words into the world. You assumed your expressions collided with one another, redundant and boring and lame, before you even got to the second retelling.

You somehow hoped speaking the words of your experience might bring back the feeling, but that was not the case. By nightfall, it seemed that calming, warm jacket was much more than that. It possessed a certain power. Wearing it created momentum in you, circulating through the nerves and arteries in your body, lighting up every inch of your being like an electric circuit that was not fully connected before. You felt a chill without it. A nakedness. The buzz of being in a flow state, the desire to want to contribute, to share, to help—all of that fizzed away.

It was that night, a couple days ago, when you remembered the words of the therapist you used to see bi-weekly.

"There's no such thing as a bad feeling. Or a good feeling, for that matter. The way in which the mind adds value to something that just is, that is a source of curiosity. Why are we latching on to it as being bad or good rather than just allowing it to be what it is?"

The therapist had sought to help you process your past, but you'd not trusted them so easily and never shared your full story. You weren't sure if you knew the full story anymore, anyway, and yet, its murky details still gnawed at you, a mold eating away the ripened fruit of your youth, contaminating one quadrant of your life at a time like a box of sullied berries. It was around then you'd noticed the neuroses. The incessant fingernail peeling. The nostril scraping. The way you'd jab your tongue at the places in your mouth that irritated you, knowing they'd irritate you more if you continued to prod them. And you'd continue to prod them. A bad feeling that felt good to induce. A means of control, at least.

"I just want to get rid of all these bad thoughts," you told the therapist in one session back then. "And get to the good ones . . . at least, more often."

"Bad and good are just the hue, the lens added like a screen over your experience by someone else's value system," they'd said.

"Who else's value system could I possibly be living by but my own?"

"I'm not sure. Maybe it's the voices of your parents, dictating what it is you *should* feel, or maybe there's a part of you that has something valuable to say, but its way of saying it drowns out the other parts of you."

You'd been stumped, trying to sit in the possibility they were right, even as you wanted to say they were wrong. That voice, the one that came from your parents, was speaking loudly, dominating the headspace. Yet, simultaneously, there was another voice whispering, "Hi? Hello? Can you hear me? I am trying to say something too."

"But my question to you is this," your therapist had said. "Who or what was at the source of that *should*? And what are they wanting to say? What are their needs?"

You weren't sure if that was a question you were supposed to respond to or not. But it was confusing to recognize there was a dominant voice in your head, drowning out other voices but still forcing you to go out of your way to listen. *Why?*

"To help answer that, I want you to try something right now," the therapist had said, asking you to sit up. "Take a deep breath, exhale it, open your mouth, and say the word for every feeling that you're experiencing right now."

You did as you were instructed. The therapist genuinely seemed to care and always had new activities to try, but none of them seemed to work. This feeling freestyle appeared frivolous. You told the therapist as much afterward.

"That's fine that you feel that way," they'd said. "But why don't you try it again when you go home? This time, try whispering the feelings to yourself out loud. If you want to try it when you're feeling particularly resistant to the moment you're in, all the better."

Years had passed. You'd given so little thought to your therapeutic experience. Then, looking out the small rectangular window at a crescent moon on a particularly clear night, where the vastness of the desert appeared more desolate and barren than the open canvas it had seemed, when you arrived, the exercise came to you.

Of course, you didn't try it right away. You pushed back. You resisted. You grabbed your phone. You sought to find some other thing to distract yourself with, firing up your social media apps. Except, the trailer you're renting has no Wi-Fi. You hadn't cared when you booked it, riding high as you were on the captain training regimen of no internet. But now, you wished you had it. You have a few bars of cell service but no data. Ages ago, you'd downloaded an offline version of Tetris. Organizing digital pieces of various shapes into straight lines sounded great. So you played until your eyes hurt, then went to sleep.

The next day, things only got worse. The metal feeling in your throat got hotter and clunkier. Even when you avoided lengthy conversations with people out in the shopping areas you visited to get a taste of regular life, you still ran into situations where you had to speak. In those moments, the tunnels connecting your brain to your voice box to your throat to your lips seemed to be covered in that boiling mix of tar and gravel. By nighttime, back in the bed, facing the window, Tetris wasn't going to cut it.

And so, you said your feelings out loud but to yourself.

"I feel wretched. I feel phony. I feel upset. I feel like my ceremonial experiences are putting me under pressure to move, but I feel slow. I feel hot. Hot. Hot. Crazy. Lame. Delirious. Absurd. Hilarious. I feel funny. Funny. Funny. Funny. And now I'm sitting in an old airstream trailer, without access to Wi-Fi, alone, in the middle of the desert, saying my feelings."

By the end of it, you were laughing at the whole escapade. Hysterically. You had found a random sign on the street, taped onto a door, walked through said door, found a book, followed its instructions, went to a strange woman's house and stared at her, drove up into the mountains to have smoke blown in your face, and high-tailed it to the desert to meet up with your ex and made perfume. It was undeniably hilarious, but you kept on.

Right away, you felt better. The tar and gravel in your throat smoothed itself into a freshly paved road, bringing about a transportive sort of non-attachment to the emotions, a passing by. It wasn't an escape but an exercise that allowed you to see the grander journey taking place, and its hilarity. You slept as well as you had during your days creating the scent with Tina and woke up refreshed and hilarious.

I'm out here in the desert, having all these thoughts about this journey. And that's cool, but at the end of the day, I'm just a rock, shifting and grow-

ing in ways that have nothing to do with the internal voices but that are happening because I am a part of nature, and water and air are moving through me.

The last thing you wanted to do was end the journey. It had been far too entertaining for that. Plus, you felt like you were learning something, even if it was only the ability to reach back into the past and make use of the stuff that had already entered your life. If that was the primary skill of a captain, like grabbing the mop and bucket out of the closet to swap the decks, then so be it.

So you cracked open the book for the first time in over a week and found this on the next page:

- *Ceremony Three: The Whisper of Life, The Screams of Death—listen to these sounds and feel the rhythm of the ocean in your blood, whether it's hot or cold.*
  - Click this hyperlink on your cell phone (yes, we know we told you not to use your phone, and yes, we know you've still been using it).

You clicked. You followed the map. This is how you've found yourself here, outside this compound, trying to whisper into submission the loud voices of resistance protesting inside you.

"I feel grounded but confused. Dark, stupid, not worthy. I feel scared. Yes, I feel scared. Scared and worried. Worried? I feel worried. I feel trapped. Unclear. I feel confused. And resigned. I feel kind of okay about it. I feel gentle. Joyful. I feel listened to. I feel kind of cheeky. Calm. I feel calm. Yeah, I feel calm."

Uttering each feeling out loud is like pressing a fast-forward button. The words scoot you away from what happened five days ago, five hours ago, fifty minutes ago, five minutes ago, and finally, five seconds ago, and forward into the exact moment.

The presence of a dozen or so other people in the lonely expanse of the desert is a comfort. After feeling the full force of your whispered feelings, you enter the compound. At its center, the space the entire operation seems to revolve around is a large domed hut with one small entrance. It looks like a desert igloo. Next to it, a blazing fire rages as an attendant looks on, feeding wood into the flames. It's like a cross between a pizza oven and a crematorium, with smoke billowing out of the chimney into the high-noon broad daylight.

"Please," says Yvonne, who introduces herself as the master of this ceremony. "Line up here to be cleansed."

Out of a smoking clay cauldron, Yvonne lifts a torch of palo santo and copal and motions the first individual in the line to stand on a brick platform covered by a bed of green herbs and surrounded by a small ring of lemons, mangos, and conch shells. She has them close their eyes. Yvonne waves the palo santo and some other smoking substance you can't discern over the participant's body, asking them to turn around and then enter the domed hut, which she refers to as a "temescal." Yvonne whispers messages throughout, but you're too far away to hear what she's saying. It sounds like gibberish.

You watch each of the participants, one by one, face a spectrum of fear, confusion, jitteriness, bravado, grins, and glee. You're the last one to receive your cleansing smoke. As you're being cleansed, you realize the whispers of Yvonne aren't gibberish at all but detailed instructions.

"You are going to want to leave. You are going to want to end it; you are going to want the journey to be over," she says. "But if you stay with it, if you stay in, perhaps you'll find what you're looking for."

Once the cleansing is complete, you crawl through the small entrance and take your seat alongside the others in a tightly packed circle. The heat is intense, and the noises inside the room sound amplified, like a recording studio made of stone, dirt, rock, water, and human bodies.

Where the other ceremonies have felt a little appropriative, from the beginning, this one feels like a more serious ceremonial space—more closely linked with native land, like those of you here on the inside have few differences from the cactus, rocks, and vegetation that poke through the desert outside. You feel you've crossed a border, not between countries but between those who care about the natural world and those who destroy it without consideration though we're a part of it.

You follow the lead of the others. When you are passed a bowl filled with the earthy mixture, it's impossible not to feel a reverence for the sacred contents. You sit for a moment with it, the crudeness of the bowl resting delicately in your hands like an offering. You carefully smear the smooth material all over your body until it covers every reachable surface. Some of those around you have covered even their faces. Moving naturally, you gently streak lines of the mixture across your forehead and down your cheeks as well.

Eventually, Yvonne crawls in behind you, with a water jug in her hand. Her ivory teeth are the last things you see before she calls for the assistant to close the door.

***

Nothing prepares you for this heat. It's thick, almost solid. With every passing second, a growing pressure gives you the sensation that you're plunging further down into the depths of an ancient, cosmic sea.

Crammed so snugly inside with other bodies, you have no space to sit cross-legged. You're forced, like your fellow participants, to hug your knees close to your chest like a fetus. Apart from the toothpick-thin lines from the outside world around the door's edges and a small hole way up at the top of the temescal, the only visible light is the haunting orange-red glow of the coals at the center of the room.

Thick with the scent of laboring human bodies, the room smells pungent and alive. Your legs and hands, already slick with sweat, press up against the limbs of your fellow ceremony attendees. It's like you're one mass, melting together into a more malleable form. The sticky friction between you and these total strangers feels natural, correct even, with no need for apology or feelings of encroachment. For every micro adjustment made, ten thousand other discomforts go unnoticed as anticipation rises.

With nothing to look at and no place for your body to stretch out, you turn your focus inward, to your breath. Your inhales have a cooling effect on the increasing heat, even if you can't tell whether the cold relief is real or imagined. After a few minutes, once the mud on your skin has started to harden, Yvonne speaks.

"In ancient times, warriors would enter the temescal after the battles had ended, and it was time to return to civilian life," she says. "They needed to be reborn in the womb of the temescal."

You concentrate on the words churning out of her mouth between the breaths, sighs, gulps, and pants echoing around the room.

"Today's ceremony will retrace the same ancient patterns that rebirthed these Indigenous warriors. Some will find the warrior within; some will find ancestors, and some will find all of that, dancing with the cosmos and stirrings our language has no words for. We will walk through four doors, *cuatro puertas*, representing the seasons, in line with the ritual of the Southern tribes, the people to whom I belong."

Her voice is like a bass drum, rhythmic and low. Each word and phrase is suspended in the air until replaced by the next. "But before we begin, I want to remind you we will be opening a portal between the living and the dead. Do not be afraid when the ghosts of our ancestors enter this space. Honor them. Respect them. Welcome them. Soon, like all who pass through this life, we, too, will be joining them on the other side."

Before Yvonne completes those words, a faint drumming begins. It is a hollow but familiar sound. Each snap of her fingers, each crash of her finger pads, collides with the surface in a way that, if you hadn't seen her bring it in, you'd struggle to place the material. Where Marlene had found a traditional Aztec drum in the musical portion of her ceremony, Yvonne opted for the plastic water jug as her instrument of percussion.

As she cracks the drum into a rhythm, she sings. Her introductory words seem more planned and pointed, but the phrasing of the song is looser, more improvised, and meandering like it's searching for something. She welcomes the ancestors. She invites them to witness the birth—your birth—into this world. She thanks them for their patience and offers gratitude to the motherly spirit that brought you all into the world. She gets graphic in her wandering lyrics, describing the blood and body fluid that comes with new life.

"The warm wetness you feel now, that is the lifeblood of your birth," she chants, fading in and out of any discernable song structure. "The hot blood of life."

As the temperature increases, your concentration dissipates. You fidget more and breathe less. You struggle and squirm. Yvonne breaks from playing the drum to pour water from a nearby bucket onto the coals. Thick plumes of steam cloud the room. The mud on your body feels greasier with every passing moment.

"The runny material on your arms is that gift from your mother, who got it from her mother, and all the way back to your oldest ancestors," Yvonne chants. "Savor it while you can because it, too, will soon fall away, and only its memory will remain."

Yvonne sings a few more lines. Your mind mixes them up, not exactly following the story. It feels like the disturbances in your body are chopping up the meaning of the words as you hear them. It's getting hard to think clearly. She sings of how your body, now born into the world, and the material that is you are all just part of a cycle, with neither a real beginning nor an end. Instead, it represents a point on a continuum that's to be celebrated and appreciated for the sheer beauty of the unique expression that is you.

"And so, you are both unique and not at all unique," Yvonne sings, slapping the plastic bucket in tandem with her voice. "An echo. An echo. An echo. An echo with its own vibration but an echo all the same."

With that, she stops playing and calls on her assistant to open the door.

When the light splashes back into the temescal, it's so bright, you have to close your eyes. For a moment, a heavenly breeze of external air blows through, refreshing you in a way you thought a hot desert afternoon never could. You narrowly open your eyelids and discover almost all the mud has been washed off through the course of the first phase.

A wooden bowl filled with salt is passed your way, and you see the other attendees rubbing lumps of the white crystals all over their bodies to prepare for the second phase. You follow their lead, rubbing salt on your sweaty, dirty body. Someone advises the group members to avoid putting the salt on their faces. Clumps of it stick to your skin as your eyes finally adjust to the light and you gaze around the room. Men and women, young and old, groups and solo adventurists like yourself comprise the participants. A few wear smirks of enjoyment, like the faces of those who love the exhilaration of roller coasters. Others carry that unmistakable look of dread, even terror.

Yvonne's assistant arrives with a shovel and some burning orange stones.

"Between every door, we add seven more," Yvonne says. "And each time we add one, we will greet our ancestors with the word *abuelita*."

The assistant adds the first stone.

"Abuelita!" the room cries out as he tips the stone into the center circle of the room.

Another stone before, "Abuelita!" And another. "Abuelita!"

Yvonne sprinkles bits of an amber material on top of the stone pile, a seemingly sacred, glowing dust. "This copal is the incense of our tribe and every tribe the world over, the contribution of all trees. The essence."

The coals are stacked so high; it seems there's a serious danger that some could fall, burning your feet. Yvonne doesn't bat an eye. She slinks back into the room once her assistant departs. They mutter a few undiscernible words to each other outside, and you briefly imagine some sinister plot to burn all of you alive. No, you are not past the point of humoring these daymares. Still, you've committed to stay, and even as Yvonne returns and grins and tells you again that if you need to leave the temescal at any time, you are welcome to, part of you knows already: you're in this for the long haul. The experiences with Marlene and Adolf woke you up to your ability to stretch, be flexible, raise your consciousness, and be aware.

This ceremony with Yvonne will be fine. I will stay for the duration. I will greet the warrior within, whose footsteps I feel approaching.

The door closes again. Right away, the temperature feels like it has tripled from the worst of it just moments ago. You take a long inhale, feeling the heat from the room rush into your lungs. You remind yourself of what the book told you this ceremony was going to be.

"The whisper of life, the screams of death. Listen to these sounds and feel the rhythm of the ocean in your blood, whether it's hot or cold."

The taste of salt permeates the air in the temescal as Yvonne begins to drum again. It's like you're at sea, on a ship sailing for Hell itself. You inhale, you exhale. You try not to think about the heat.

Yvonne's voice, less singing now than wailing, ricochets around the room. Its sharpness digs into those places where the salt rubs into scrapes and irregularities in your skin.

"Life is not easy. It's not clear; it's full of pain and suffering with no answers or reasons," she says. "The ancestors remain with us, but now they sit on the sidelines, calling out their instructions, and we do not listen."

It feels like your skin is cooking, the salt-like seasoning for soon-to-be crispy, savory sheets of human flesh. Beneath it, your blood bubbles like a hot soup below a blow torch. Your pattern of breathing is interrupted so regularly that it's hard to string together more than a few gasps at a time. You hear others struggling to contain their discomfort too.

"While we're alive, we so often want life to be over!" Yvonne screams in a way that proves she's in this room too, enduring this same heat. "It's too painful, too uncomfortable to bear. It's too pointless to be worth such devastation."

For the first time, the thought of leaving slices through your mind.

I am uncomfortable. I can't do this. I will fail.

You wade through the sweltering desert of these thoughts, desperate for relief.

"I can't," a voice says. At first, you think the voice belongs to you. But the man speaks again. "I can't keep going! I need to go out. Let me out."

Yvonne quits drumming and calls her assistant. You can hear the muffled words coming in a comforting tone, of a woman's voice, seemingly begging him to stay. He rejects her.

"Open the door," Yvonne says loudly.

Still, no one arrives. A sense of panic, of being trapped in the fiery space, permeates the room.

"Let me out!" the man cries, now fumbling forward through the darkness. The sound of wet limbs colliding is the only rhythm in the room now that Yvonne's drumming has stopped.

"I need to go out. I can't breathe."

Suddenly, you feel like you can't breathe, either. Maybe you need to leave too.

Maybe we all do.

Yvonne clears her throat, "Open the . . ."

Finally, the door slides open, and the man clambers over the last few people sitting between him and the exit, escaping to the outside. From your position near the door, you close your eyelids instead of tempting yourself with a glance outward. Further inward you go, encouraging yourself.

I hear the warrior's footsteps. They are growing louder!

You try to beat back the jealousy that bubbles up. Jealousy that this man had the courage to leave this foolishness behind. Jealous of his conviction to quit.

The door closes again.

"We've only just begun to open the second door," Yvonne announces to a concert of grumbles and sighs. "And we will keep going, in search of the warrior."

Again, the chanting begins. Again, the temperature rises to unbearable thresholds. You assumed having one less person in this crowded space would afford an inch or two of extra room for your body, but the abandoned space has already been commandeered by someone sitting cross-legged.

How sweet that bit of relief must feel.

Like a dozen little chimneys, you picture your fellow participants sucking in air and blowing out steam. Their mouths and lungs push and pull the hot oxygen around the room like a desperate, hurried, unorganized school band. There's no beauty in these sounds, only the ugliness of voluntary suffering. If only you were alone in here. Maybe then you could concentrate on your breath. You could lie down. You could listen and look inward.

Running out of options to distract yourself, you pinch sections of your body with your fingernails. You grit your teeth and clamp down on the soft parts of your thigh until that pain is as intense as the heat. Then you stop, wait for the heat to take over as your primary enemy, and begin to pinch elsewhere.

"Oh, dear ancestors," Yvonne chants. "What is the reason for this life's pain?"

The appeal of the pinching wears off. You have no idea how long it bought you. Time vanishes in this darkness. You rub your eyes and instantly regret it—you'd forgotten about the salt. The salt you'd already applied though someone recommended not to.

Shoot. Shoot. Shoot.

The salt burns in a more pointed, fiercer way than the heat's slow squeeze. You hate yourself for the salt and for staying. You feel like a fool for seeking something in yourself that doesn't exist. Shame rears its ugly head.

How can I find the light in myself when covered in all this darkness?

Yvonne plays the water jug drum. You sway, trying to shake the pain away. You're the type to dance around the room on one foot when you stub your toe. Now it's both your body and mind that feel stubbed.

"And those deepest pains of life," Yvonne says. "They do not go away. Not while we're alive, maybe not afterward, either."

Dizziness comes as some tension leaves your body. You've given up the fight unconsciously, lost in this bodily sway. You feel, sense, taste, and smell nothing. Your eyes are slammed shut. Your body is wet and sloppy, and your butt is numb from sitting. You sway to Yvonne's drums and leave your body behind.

You travel back to the shame, but you are not you. You are only the torrent of desperation, confusion, and eagerness others see in your eyes. You beg yourself to stop. You don't.

"And life will not let up, so we must ask," Yvonne says. "Can we fight the pain forever?"

You've only ever felt darkness about that day. You've never told a soul about what happened. Not your therapist, not your exes. No one.

"Can you win the fight against pain?" she sings. "Is there delight in defeat? What's the difference between victory and defeat? What's worth celebrating?

The drums grow louder.

"So scream with me now," Yvonne commands. "Just scream!"

Still out of your own body, in the watercolor mess of your memory, you scream. At yourself. At your friend. At all the screamers screaming in the temescal around you. Your anger and pain and shame join theirs. The sound waves of this screaming symphony crash against your skin.

What's that?!

It's not just sound. Out of nowhere, droplets of water splash on you. You return to your body as others pull water from some jugs and pass it around. Some gargle water and spit it out. Others pour it over their heads. You get yourself a cup. The water must be hot, but it feels cold compared to the inferno of the room.

Sweet relief.

You splash water into your eyes and blink them open. Yvonne douses the crumbling coals at the center with water. Steam cascades out.

"Open the door!" Yvonne announces.

Her assistant cracks open the hot chamber, and Yvonne stops beating her drum.

The same routine transpires over the next several minutes: hot stones, *abuelitas,* copal. This time you feel your physical body urge out the chant, *abuelita,* and normal mental processes feel like distant memories. It's like the "you" you knew has gone elsewhere. Even your pulse feels like it's rattling from deeper inside of you than what you understand as your physical anatomy.

In the light from the doorway, a bowl is passed around with pieces of a green plant inside. You are so hungry that you put it in your mouth without a second thought, spitting it out only when you see others rub its juices over their bodies.

No words are spoken. You're surrounded by locals and visitors, people who must have experienced this many times, and those uninitiated, like you; yet it's as if you're alone. No one else is in here but you. Just three shades of yourself, battling it out to be heard: the mind, the body, and the ways you distract it all by letting them fold in on themselves.

"They've arrived here on the doorstep," Yvonne says as the door shuts again. "Are you ready to let your warrior in?"

The door closes, and the song begins again. A placid stillness spreads around the temescal. An ocean of space has opened up from the intensity of the last ceremony. There is a feeling of grossness, and you sit in it and smile. Accepting it, welcoming it.

"Even the harshest seasons have their time," she sings. "The abuelitas, how do they respond to these changes? To the comings and goings of things? To intensity and calm?"

The more Yvonne plays, the more the shock from the second door floats away. It's as if the snowbanks from a cold, harsh winter melt, and bright colors poke through the frozen earth. Yellows, reds, and emerald greens—the vibrant paint swatches on a warrior's headdress.

Here, as the warrior reaches out its hand, you see its grace and beauty. Your muscles tighten; your posture straightens; your shoulders widen, and your breath remains deep, even, and unlabored. There's a soft firmness in your limbs, a flexible machinery. Like the way snow falls, freezes, melts, and returns to vapor. Here is a warrior of change who is grateful to be here.

Yvonne's voice is soft and loopy. Perhaps, you think, a curiosity flows through her. "And how do you greet someone familiar? How do you greet someone for the first time? Was there ever a difference?"

The door opens again. More stones are added to the pile. The assistant climbs in and blows a healing dust into your nose. It travels through your nostrils and cascades down the back of your throat and into your gut, dispersing into your bloodstream. Your cells lighten, a sense of calm spreading over you as your eyes water.

Roots and stems of what look like withered parsley are passed around next. They are bitter and chewy in your mouth. You gnaw into its peppery flesh and break off each bit like celery, then swallow it down.

"Oshá and rapé," Yvonne says. "These two medicines feed the newly awoken warrior. How does the warrior respond? What do they do next? Where do they go, and when do they return?"

The rhythm of her song is slow and gentle. The lava stones sit in a heaped stack in the middle of the temescal, simmering the room in a way that feels more like a campfire.

The powder and root soothe you on what feels like a molecular level. There's a soft buzzing, like goosebumps, that crawls across your skin—the container for all these pieces, this warrior, this life. Your life.

"Why do travelers celebrate so merrily when they return?" Yvonne asks in a casual, chanting cadence. "Is it because they are grateful to have survived? Or was something else learned?"

Again, you rock your body in circles. This time, you do so in a syncopated sway, easily falling into the rhythm.

"And they will die, probably sooner than they imagine. And death will come fast or slow. A sickness. An accident. A mistake. Eaten by the forces of nature. And what do they savor? How do they savor it? The ancestors who've been with us today know, don't they? Can you hear what the abuelitas are trying to tell you?"

You hear again the breaths of your fellow bathers, your fellow lodgers, sailors, participants. Their individual noises now unify, creating some bigger humming, throbbing energy. A sensation rises within you, and you open your eyes. You're all swaying in your own ways, moving and exploring the tiny spaces between your bodies. There's a sense of achievement bubbling through the group. You can hear it in the air, in the echoing acoustics of this stone studio.

"Life, even in all of its pain, is a celebration of death's imminent arrival. It's a party until death comes," Yvonne says so softly that it's more of a whisper. "Sing it with me."

She says it softly at first.

"Life is . . ."

In the space after her simple noun and verb, Yvonne produces only a sound. It's not language, per se. it's some combination of breathing, chanting, mumbling, screaming, and whispering. Almost like an accident, almost like a sound she's never uttered before. A chance utterance. It's the wisdom a warrior never speaks but always understands.

You add your voice to the chorus, "Life is . . ." and then you add your spin on it.

"Life is . . ."

Others add their sounds, joining in to create the truest noise you've ever heard.

Again, louder now, "Life is . . ." Yvonne slaps her drum harder. "Now scream it."

"Life is!"

CHAPTER 10

FAILING FORWARD

Your arms lay slack, draped alongside your legs. There's an infinite emptiness inside your stomach. You feel like a hollow stone.

Yvonne has stopped chanting. A few of your fellow sweat lodgers inhale and exhale in a kind of woodwind chime. It's as if you can hear each droplet of sweat rain down your skin in a faint pitter-patter. The searing heat has flatlined. In this pulpy air, it's as if you're all suspended in this membrane between the living and the dead, where the voices of your ancestors whisper to you, not through sound but through sensation itself.

Ancestors—your grandfather, your uncle, and their elders—come forth. One by one, you feel them, with their masks over your own. You breathe through their nostrils, taste the moisture on their lips, and blink the heavy lids over their eyes. A furry thicket of hair populates your ears like you remember investigating in those belonging to Grandfather when you were a boy. Your fingers find a stiff, granite-like jaw hardened below you, the prominent feature of your uncle in family photos. The fibers of these features connect with their opposites inside your spirit. You inhabit these men as though you were always them, even after they'd left the world of the living.

There's nothing to be said during these facial wardrobe changes, only a sense of how the after-party proceeds. A stillness. A *fiesta* frozen in place. A captured celebration without risk of being dropped and shattered. A sense of forever and forgiveness.

Inhabiting your ancestors allows you to poke around and explore further with those on other planes, walking somewhere far beyond the walls of the temescal. You honor them as yourself and honor yourself as them, for slights and insensitivities. You step into their entire bodies without moving an inch. Their skin feels much lighter on you than the sagging pain of words spoken to each other in angry haste.

The ancestors only want to protect and guide you. They only want to serve the duty bestowed upon them. They convey how they failed and how it eats at them like a disease. You don't intervene to make corrections. It's not about right or wrong, true or false. These are just spiraling colors and shapes in the kaleidoscope of present experience. You are here now, at long last, but you are not only you. You are your ancestors and your fellow guests. And you are life itself, including, not separate from, death. And death invites you to relax here in the dark, dank heat.

But you're scared.

All of you, even those in other realms, share the same stripe of fear, wearing it like a birthmark on the body. It's your unifying force. This inescapable fear vibrates on your skin like a burrowing insect, threatening to tunnel down, spiral through your bones, and burst your organs. This fear wants to be acknowledged, to be accounted for, to be fed.

An image comes into view. You're lying down in a foreign land, somewhere truly unfamiliar. Your back, and only your back, is touching this strange earth. The rest of you—legs, arms, head—do not touch the earth because these pieces are not part of you. Your limbs have been severed, leaving this lonely torso. You've expressed yourself, and it has gone too far. You've been betrayed by your own openness.

A horn blows outside the sweat lodge, rattling you back inside your living body. Immediately, you recognize the noise on a primal level. The conch shell sounds like a Viking horn. It dawns on you that the mere fact that you can discern between the two as if you've lived lifetimes on the seas, matters.

Are these even captain skills? Or are they something else?

In the last intensity of the heat, you find it. You join forces with your inner warrior. Together you detach from the immediate pain and some greater, wider pain beyond. Settling into the inner warrior's power, you gain control of how you react to the environment. Just then, the door opens for the last time, and Yvonne leads you out of the smaller container and back into the bigger one.

Your keister hurts like crazy from sitting in the sweat lodge when you finally stand up to exit. You're partially surprised you're still alive. The medicine tingles throughout your being as you and the others reemerge. On the way out, you stare at a row of cairns lining the entrance. You didn't notice them when you arrived, but you know them now.

What led me here only to miss this? What's the point of it? Did my path down the captain's road get hijacked? Was there a mutiny? Did I start to dream of a time when I'd have my own ship, when being captain itself became just another achievement? A gold star?

The stomach pain strikes again. The rumbling. The discomfort. You're not up for engaging in conversation with the other participants the way you see some of them circling up in little groups to talk about their experiences. Their eyes glow with the talk of glimpsing something spoken of in shorthand as "enlightenment."

You accept your feeling of nonacceptance. You decide it's okay not to mingle and share with the others. You realize your process will not be so linear. This isn't a figuring-it-all-out process but another range of processes. These refractory periods will continue; the resistance will mostly be resisted. Your hope is to be more attuned and self-aware, however acute or obtuse the resistances become.

Maybe I am improving in the middle of the disappointment. Maybe I am aware of that improvement. Maybe there is no outcome, no trajectory. After all, things have felt better inside when not thinking about the cherry on top.

"But the decks will always need swabbing," the voice of the warrior whispers calmly in your head. "And you can handle it. Perhaps you can even find the lesson in it."

You scramble, fall short, and fail, but you remain curious.

Does it matter who is at the helm?

This curiosity, even if you don't claim it explicitly as such, is another kind of cairn entirely—a cairn locator.

Just outside the center, you nearly race past it. You're so caught up with what is happening within—the process of being the warrior rather than becoming it—that you nearly miss your bag sitting on the ground. Or, at least, it's a bag that looks identical to yours. You thought you'd left it at the Airstream.

Did I bring it here? How'd I forget to bring it inside?

You lean down, reach inside, and pull out the book.

CHOOSE YOUR OWN ADVENTURE, OR DON'T

Warrior is speaking inside my head.

You can't skip this chapter. If you choose to break the rules, you have to go to Chapter 12. You don't get to enjoy Chapter 11 at all. I mean the real 11, not whatever the combination of Roman Numerals above conotate. I don't speak Roman Numeral and don't tell me you do either. Who'd believe it? If you do choose to participate and take a picture, we will send you a bonus code to something you won't believe.

Now, how about that for a ceremony?

I reckon at this point, you've about twisted up your noggin so many times, you could hog-tie your limbs together with its goop, pitch yourself overboard, and escape from the binds without losing a beat.

But I'm gonna have to ask you to do it again. I know . . . I know. These reflections are getting tiresome. I get it. It's just part of it, s'all I can say. Gotta trust me.

- *"Sing me a song, O muse, of the rage of captains that brought countless ills upon themselves." In other words, let's hear you sing some improvised song lyrics. Go ahead. Sing.*

***

Now, wasn't that enjoyable?

Also, if you didn't do it, that's okay too. The last thing I want you to do is to do things just to please me. You probably are used to caretaking others' needs and wants. And in that process, perhaps you lose yourself. So whatever you do or don't do, just make sure you do it for you and only you. Your primary responsibility here is to show up for yourself. So if you trusted me, I hope it was because you trusted you.

You are welcome and congratulations on completing Chapter XI!

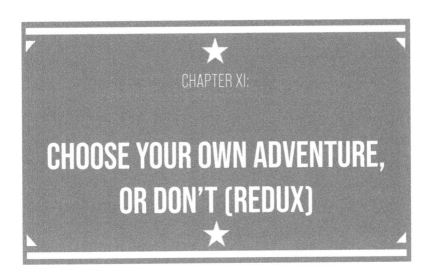

CHOOSE YOUR OWN ADVENTURE, OR DON'T (REDUX)

INT. BOOKSTORE—DOWNSTAIRS

Andy browses a bookshelf adjacent to the entrance of The Last Bookstore.

> ANDY: "I don't know, man."
> AL: "About what?"
> ANDY: "I don't see that kind of funkiness in any of these books."
> AL: "Can you be more specific?"

Andy slides a title from the shelf and flips through it, aiming the interior pages at Al like mirrors in which to view himself.

> ANDY: "Stopping the text suddenly with a weird chapter, numbered differently, to demand that readers sing impromptu, freestyle song lyrics . . ."

Al rubs his beard. Andy has no beard.

AL: "Hold up, that was your idea."
ANDY: ". . . a link to the scent mentioned in the book . . ."
AL: "That was your idea too!"

Andy grunts, plopping the book back on the shelf sideways, nowhere near the place he took it from. Then, Andy glares at Al.

ANDY: "A furry book cover featuring a book with a furry book cover as the main symbol . . ."
AL: "Okay. That was me."

The two stare at each other for a beat.

AL: "We can always scrap all that, you know? Do something more conventional."

Andy runs his hands through his hair. Al has no hair.

AL: "You have some solid, real-world work experiences. We could build it around practical advice for young people struggling to find their footing in their careers."
ANDY: "But, Al, I'd never want to read a book like that."
AL: "Me neither, but—"
ANDY: "But maybe we will scrap some of the experimentation, leave other bits in there, and even include our whole conversation about what to include and what to lose right in the text as a kind of redux."

Al clears his throat.

AL: "Hm. That's worth considering. But I have a feeling you'll end up saying you have mixed feelings about that too."

Andy shrugs.

AL: "You know there's a book labyrinth upstairs; maybe we will find our answer up there."

INT. BOOKSTORE—UPSTAIRS

Al guides Andy through an old bank vault turned Sci-Fi section, a tunnel made of books, and into several walls of books organized by color and nothing more.

ANDY: "I don't know that I'd call this a labyrinth exactly."
AL: "That's the kind of thing I would say."
ANDY: "Maybe you're rubbing off on me."
AL: "It's supposed to be the other way around."

They round the corner and find themselves in a section about China. Andy pulls another book off the shelf.

ANDY: "Here's something we can agree on."

Andy flashes the cover toward Al.

AL (Reading): "I Ching."
ANDY (Reading): "The Classic Chinese Oracle of Change."

Andy throws the book open and cycles through the pages, stopping randomly on page 310. There is a character on the page: Fu 復

ANDY (Reading): "A grid that contains all."

AL (Reading): "Controlling the structure."

ANDY (Reading): "Punishing expedition."

AL: "Ideograms can mean so many things."

Andy and Al exchange a knowing glance.

ANDY: "Exactly."

Andy closes the book and returns it to the shelf.

ANDY: "And that's everything we need to know about our book. The purpose boils down to that, like the number 42."

AL: "Wait. What?"

ANDY: "Oh nothing, just something I got a kick out of way back."

They both laugh for a moment, then continue walking before Al stops. He returns to the bookshelf, takes the book out, and puts it back with the spine facing inwards.

ANDY: "How do you know about that?"

AL: "About what?"

Andy stares at Al for an uncomfortably long time before speaking.

ANDY: "Sometimes I don't know if you are collaborating with me on this or you're an antagonist in this journey. I don't know if you're a writing assistant called Al, short for Alex, or an AI—as in, artificial intelligence—writing assistant."

AL: "Who cares?"

Both Andy and Al look at the audience as we fade out.

THE END
(of this particular scene at least, evidently)

INTEGRATING THE SHADOW

Y ou slide off your sandals. Moist, freshly cut grass caresses your bare feet. Your heels and toes are soon covered in green sawdust of mulchy shrapnel and delicate blades. Rumbles of a lawnmower growl in the distance, slowly vanishing from the public park as early morning gives way to full-blown daytime.

You've been sitting here for just a few minutes, but the dampness from the bench has absorbed through to your underwear. It's just tolerable enough to not regret wiping the surface down before you sit. Though, there are far more important things to consider, to train yourself not to worry about.

A man about thirty feet from you struggles to manage his trident of exotic birds. One is bright yellow, another red, and a third blue. They toggle back and forth on his arms like turrets on a fortress wall, multicolored weapons ready to be deployed at the joggers and dog walkers that orbit the main grassy area. Many of them, like you, have to do a double take to make sure their eyes aren't deceiving them. Perhaps they also thought they were coming to a city park on a regular morning, only to find themselves at a circus.

And it seems I've come to provide the soundtrack.

Having finally made it back to the city after some more obscure social interactions in the mountains and desert, you find civilization has lost some of its appeal. Even as the birdman sends his parrots—are they parrots?—out for their first swooping flights and passersby meander toward the spectacle with phones drawn, there's less rumination about whether these people are going to judge you, wiggling your feet back and forth as you are on the freshly cut grass.

Since leaving the desert, you've tried to make an honest assessment of where you've gone so far and how much further you're willing to go, but now you let your non-thinking self take over. You find your body guides you to play a song from your phone, "Niger" by Malian Musicians and Damon Albarn. The beat, coupled with the sounds of the birds, reminds you of that moment of pride you had during that long drive when you naturally freestyled on top of some of your favorite African beats. And again, you just start riffing.

"Every time my heart settles in, I find myself. The sound of the birds, the beautiful sights. Here we are. Here I am. I came with a message to deliver. Now I want to have you hear it, to see it, to feel it."

You repeat: "I want you to hear what I have to say."

This allows you to witness a little of your self-doubt creep in as some passersby stop and listen to what must seem to be *some crazy person.* But then another thought occurs.

Yeah. Maybe what is crazy is living your life thinking that someone who is doing something creative and scary is crazy.

The more you think, the more the words start to flow. The idea of being crazy, the idea that you are part of some bizarre spectacle—what does that mean?

How can we all break free if I am the crazy person? Then comes the judgment of the feeling, but what I am doing isn't a product. That's what must change so that more can be allowed.

"Let my flow, let my being, let my sad, let my love flow. It is that flow that cures, the flow that liberates, the flow that lets us be us. The flow that heals, the flow that has us return to ourselves and who we are, who we are meant to be."

It's odd how some words are coming out and others are staying in because you aren't controlling anything, and you see how, in the moments you become more aware, you stumble.

"You see, every time I become aware of you, I stumble. The key to my heart is staying in it, without anything from beyond except the trees, the plants, the birds. We are put here to listen, but it gets confusing—what we should listen to. So I come back to myself; I lose my thoughts, and I come back. I come back. I come back."

You open up your eyes, and there's a drummer who stopped by—maybe a couple of minutes ago—someone you don't know, who started drumming along with you.

You're not a musician. You can't sing. And you haven't ever, as far as you can remember, harbored some deep desire to want any musical skill. You've simply asked yourself, reflecting on your last ceremony, a simple question about the role of music on a ship: *What good would a captain be without a jolly singing voice?*

A good chuckle follows as you think of it now, just as what happened then. By now, you've accepted the absurdity of this whole live-performance art thing you've been inhabiting the last couple of weeks.

On your drive back from the desert, precisely at 2:37 in the morning, you started listening to a Spotify station based on one of your favorite songs, "Donsolu" by BKO Quintet from *The Many Are One* beating drum compilation. What followed was a set of random, pan-African jazz, modern beats that inspired you to be your own troubadour, adding your meandering soul's spoken word on top of the beats. You remember judging your voice, how it didn't sound traditionally good. But there was a flow, a space that just seemed to melt away time. The words spilled out of your mouth. You were an observer, watching your flow as you drove around sharp turns from a place of experience. You were impressed and proud.

At some point, you switched on the recording function on your phone, only to hear the music stop playing. Apparently, technology hasn't evolved yet to allow for simultaneous playing and recording on the phone. You went back to singing or speaking or rapping, whatever it is that you want to call it. It sounded good, and you wanted to share it with the world.

But when? How? Would people like it? Reject it? Why does it matter if they do or don't? Screw it. Why not try to put these things out there? I think it's good. What if people like it? And if they don't, then who cares? Should I really record this?

But then you realized you didn't know how to download the right editing software. And what if you can only do it between 2 and 3 a.m. when the window to the subconscious is open? Maybe that would be cool, to wake up and record every day at that time. Maybe that would be your creative process.

This is the part you've enjoyed the most, watching your expectations melt away. You've long thought serious things are the only things worth doing and that they are meant to be taken seriously. And now, you find yourself opting for play if given the choice, even when you're in distress. That distress, you've reckoned, has grown into a collection of heavy luggage. You've dragged it around. You've taken it with you through the parade of serious doings in your life ever since childhood faded away. Fun, the very thing people know you for, over the last few years became nothing but a cart to make the luggage shuttling a bit easier. You could stack all the bags on top, then proceed to drink and drug and dance yourself silly enough to get back to a sense of childhood play. Only then would you have the gall to send the whole thing careening down the stairs. Only then would you have the courage to be free.

And if life is . . . what's the use in trying to define it so seriously?

At least that's what you wrote about in your reflection, the first song you've composed since you were a child writing poems in crayon on paper, with lines so wide you felt you could stuff the whole world between them. It's those words you've come here to the park to sing now. You may have made progress on your flexibility to break social conventions, but you're not exactly impervious to public embarrassment. Before you begin freestyling as Chapter XI of your copy of the furry book prompted, you close your eyes. And breathe.

"I happily spent time on my knees, prayin' to porcelain gods for peace."

Your voice is a little more than regular conversation level. You easily hear the squawking of the exotic birds and regular park chatter over yourself.

"And gladly let the play button roll through another dozen episodes."

You open your eyes. No one besides the drummer remains. So you turn it up a few decibels.

"What a joy it is watching the dice, kiss the felt of the table just right.

"And to shake the chips in my pocket . . . lightning . . . a fork in a socket."

With no further reactions from the park crowd, you close your eyes again. And scream it.

"Gyrations and vibrations! On the prowl for skin and the next vacation!"

Your heart is beating harder now, and you open your eyes. You belt it.

"Vibrations low and high . . . sensations fast and slow . . .

"Pull me to different skies . . . pull me inside out, so . . .

"Soiled my pants, my naked dance, my freedom . . .

"But only at first glance."

A kid in a stroller is staring at you. Her—his?—mom is on a cell phone, paying you no mind. Only the eyes of the child meet yours. The rest of the park visitors do their thing or watch the birds do theirs.

It's remarkable how small of a dent your performance made in this mid-morning park drama. And even though the words feel good as they pour out of you, the sensation of another comfort zone widening is something else too. Something more disturbing, hiding in the words you utter, that wouldn't quite pop out if they were just lying prone on the page as writing.

Your pants feel recently soiled, and not just because of the bench's dewy surface you sat on. Pouring out these feelings leaves you spilled out. A lump of jelly on a sliver of the toast that is your consciousness. You dislike, more than a little, these frivolous confessions disguised as art, and you reprimand yourself accordingly.

You slide on your sandals, stand up, and attempt to shove the whole feeling back into the knapsack whence it came. But it squiggles away and snakes behind you as you walk toward the park's small pond, treating the path toward it as a plank, rigid in your movements like a piece of shiplap.

You get to the pond and gaze into the water. Looking back at you is not your reflection as you expect it. It's a darker figure. You can't see the features of your face clearly, only the outline of the space you take up in the world—a tracing of the matter that comprises your reflected shape.

Someone sees you from the other side of the pond. They watch you stare down at the water. This is not the first time they're seeing you, nor will it be the last. Today, they decide to come over and introduce themselves.

When they enter your field of vision, you give them a once-over and scoot away from them. They don't get the hint. They step toward you, drifting closer. Their clothes are thick but tattered. A dank smell floats as they draw near. They occupy another space than the one you've come to know as your own—like they are in another dimension. The moment you have this thought, you sense that they know you're having it.

Because I've seen them before, haven't I?

"You've seen me before, haven't you?" Their voice is syrupy and slow.

Woman? Man? Can't tell.

"Why didn't you invite me in for tea?"

"In where?" you ask, your eyes fixed on the pond.

"In the gap between the buildings, where someone has fashioned some collected things in a space of their own," they continue. "Cardboard castle, throne of old coats, pillows of bundled plastic bags, shopping cart steed—the whole package."

Wait . . .

"You're the drifter of *Captains Wanted* fame." Your words sound accusatory.

"Only the drifter is in sight, dragging along a newly salvaged wood pallet along the sidewalk," they say. "You admired my castle and my new drawbridge, but when I opened my door, you had vanished. Why?"

You don't feel the wheels in your head turning. Nor do you notice the fidgety movements of your tongue and teeth when the words form. The words simply empty from you, lyrics to a song you've never had to learn.

"Because I'm so full of myself, and when I looked at you, I felt a sort of uncomfortable guilt. You're an outcast with a history that is behind you and a future that might not be that different from your murky past. Now there's nowhere for you to live but an unknown hopeless place, and I need hope, possibility. A future. I need it like air. I'm addicted to a chance to be something, to accumulate wealth and status, to leave a positive impact on the world, to not die a failure or as a mediocre being. You're disgusting to look at, to smell. I don't want to look at you. You drift from place to place, with no one to love you, and I am not even sure you want to live. You live in the depths, the grime, and wallow in the purged detritus of the rest of the world. I feel sorry for you, and it pains me to look you directly in your eyes. It's way easier for me to make you out to be some sort of boogie man, and I'm afraid your disgustingness and bad luck might rub off on me."

"And here I was going to tell you that I think you're doing a great job, you arse," they say.

"Hearing from you that I'm doing a great job isn't good enough. It just makes me feel worse."

"So what?" they ask. "You want a different life? You don't want to be me?"

"Of course, I've got regrets. Who doesn't? I don't want to be you, and I am afraid of that. Of being an afterthought, of dying alone, of dying feeling like I didn't do anything with my life. And yes, I want a different life than this. Who would want to run around like a psycho, following some furry book's random advice? Who would want to sing nonsense in the middle of a park and then get into a conversation with someone like you in your sad state? I should have bolted when I had the chance when I smelled you coming."

"Don't kid yourself, buddy," they say. "I was already here. Always."

The drifter drifts away again, and you're left pulling at the quickly elongating magnetic tape of your thoughts, like the ribbon uncoiling from an old, broken video tape. This frightens you and you try to look away from the lake. You close your eyes to get away.

There was a dream once, where you were in the depths of a mountain with many passages. You walked in, closed the door behind you, and found a mirror in those depths. Looking back at you was a ghoul, a dark green version of yourself with boils all over its face, all filled with puss. Some were dripping and covering the bare chest of this creature, which you knew was some version of you. You tried to look away, but instead, you went into a trance state and began to move your body in some sort of ecstatic, perverse flow. You had become this creature of your mind and you slithered to various corners of the room, salivating at the mouth, coming across different moments in your life where you traveled into these far recesses of the ground. There were those drunken sexual escapades, the lying to partners to get something you wanted, the dark dirty thoughts you tried to push away.

Eyes still closed, a long gangly laugh pours out of you, reminding you of how you used humor to cover up these moments you were ashamed of. The breadcrumbs of darkness were ignored by a story you told yourself and others, but those crumbs were all there, soaking up the puss dripping from your chin. Nothing would make these thoughts go away. You see flashes of these moments. Moments that would make others want to purge themselves of the memories you had caused.

Now you, right there next to the lake, purge. You vomit and release the memories of times when you had caused pain and suffering. You remember moments where pain had been inflicted on you. Times you were violated. Times when your space was penetrated, demolished, broken. And as you see the familiar faces of these demons from the past, their vomit flows from your mouth as you purge for their sins. You are the vessel for their grime and they for yours. The cycle of pain. The *we all are in this together*. That we are all demons to ourselves and others. This is what you find down here. What *we* find down here.

In badly wanting this to go away, you slap your sandals along the path toward what looks like a control panel at the edge of the lake. A sign nearby describes this recreation area as a former waste management site, repurposed a few decades earlier for recreation.

We're literally in the crap. Or, I guess, what used to be crap.

And nothing has changed, has it?

You reflect on the feeling you had when you left the interview just a couple weeks back now. There was a lot of pain and judgment, but it didn't feel as abysmal and icky as this septic tank tourism. Worse still, back then, you had some anchor in society's expectations; now you've gone completely unhinged. What are you meant to bind yourself to? What points the way?

Where are the blasted cairns?

And then you see her.

She's gorgeous. A neat dress. Her skin is sparkling. Her body, curvy, with a smile as radiant as the sunlight. She's flipping through the pages of an old paperback on a blanket, with her heels stored neatly to the side.

Every limb in your body slacks on your torso like dead meat. You feel like a hollowed-out shell. And somehow, you find yourself suddenly called to life—this sprout of desire that's so visceral that you feel it in the back of your throat. A clawing.

There is one version of what happens next. One dream, imagined.

You collect yourself and head back toward your car, knowing you have to pass the woman as you go. Your sexual realities nip at your feet as you walk. A burning desire for physical contact makes you feel more ashamed than anything up to this point. You feel how out of control your sexuality makes you. You pull out of the park and drive, this desire sitting shotgun to meet someone for sex, to touch yourself, to watch porn, to disappear into some sexual pause from this shame, even if you know it only will make you feel more ashamed by seeking it in a dark spirit. The city spreads out before you and draws you into its embrace, this pull toward a more satisfying numbing. The self-soothing appeal of an orgasm is to hide the need to belong, to not feel alone. This is the part of the shadow you choose to cozy up against. Your favorite escape. Relief. An end to this.

But instead of all that backward regression, instead of going down, something else arises. The warrior's attention is drawn elsewhere.

Forward. Up.

It's a song you've never heard. Or maybe you've heard it hundreds of times but never listened to it before. It's a squawking. A cry or a call. You don't decide which; you just take it in. The sounds are so beautiful that your eyes drift away from the woman on the blanket as you walk—and not just the woman but the spiral of the old habit and pattern, the lower energetic ways of dealing with the pain and loneliness. You stop walking, and your eyes go to the bird dancing around in the tree above her.

Explosive pink flowers light up the crown of the tree like a fireworks show. Its wild, untamed trunk consists of sharp brown spikes on its deep green skin. A tingling sensation, like goosebumps, trinkles up your spine and spreads down your limbs. Shuffling around on the branch is a bright green bird, opening its mouth and singing out. It's like your ears have been split open—a machete on a coconut. The song echoes loud enough to drown out the distant hum of traffic, the voices of nearby children playing. An eye points in your direction as you stand, arrested, looking at what appears to be a parrot.

A flood of similarly dressed birds arrives in a cascade of sounds— loud sirens and gentle chirps, screams and whistles. Within seconds, a dozen green and yellow parrots fill the tree. It's a miracle.

You sit down, right there, cross-legged, and stare.

After some time watching the creatures play, sing, and feast on pod fruits, you collect yourself. You nearly fall as you stand, not able to take your eyes off the birds. You continue to marvel and proceed forward as if you're pulled magnetically toward the tree and the grove beyond it.

The woman has disappeared.

CHAPTER 12

EMBRACING AND SHARING THE POWER

Waves of light surge through your body as curiosity gives way to hope and wonderment, like all the bright colors on the tapestry in the tree that lie within you as well. A serene sense of being valued and loved washes over you like a warm blanket. The rays of late afternoon splash against you, the trees, the birds, and the blossoming flowers at divine angles.

As you make your way past the first tree and onward through the grove, you take in all the differences. Some of the tree trunks are tall, smooth, and straight; others bend and twist, the bark rough and jagged. But you linger on none of them, judge none of them.

You come across a single bush exploding with colorful flowers. Yellow and white, red and pink. You're drawn to a purple flute-shaped batch and run your fingers through the petals. It's as if the grooves of your fingerprints can detect the pulsing, vibrant life right here, right now.

Like when you've stared into a kaleidoscope long enough, you doze off. You're still aware of the park but less aware of your own presence. A brief thought occurs that you are unsafe, that you can't control your body. Then a voice quickly enters and speaks to you.

"You are safe. You are safe enough to love and to dream and to breathe. You are safe now to give and receive love. *You are safe now to give and receive love.*"

There's a cozy tingly feeling in your body, and what you see around you is what you saw before—when you were fully awake. You know that, but now, in this moment, the perspective is different. You're pleasantly curious about this perspective. It's as if your formless body and the tree around you have meshed, and as you float, dictated by where you focus your energy, you become the very thing the energy has shifted toward. In this state, as the tree, you see a part of you, an acorn, fall to the ground, and you are struck by the stillness of the acorn's descent. There's a sadness, but not a sadness with a negative hue. It's more like a bittersweet goodbye. But even that can't describe the full expression of the lack of value being placed on the acorn. You are aware of how you are noticing the subtle lack of attachment to the sadness as being neither good nor bad.

The acorn lands. Quickly, a young squirrel swoops in to snatch it. There is a palpable joy for the squirrel and the acorn, but it's a joy that doesn't come with an attachment. The joy is more like that of an observer, in a peaceful witness of life's delicate balance. Perhaps that is the emotion you are witnessing: a welcoming of what is.

And again, you become aware of the potency of this realization that comes from outside the dream, outside the mind. The awareness of these emotions isn't attached to a good or bad narrative until it's put into words. Here, in this space of silent observation, what is, is. And what is shown is just the raw delicate balance effortlessly taking place outside of the sense of control you normally have—outside the story. Your focus remains on the place on the ground where the acorn fell. The top part of the acorn, where it had been attached to the tree, remains on the ground like a hat someone dropped and forgot to pick back up.

Just a form changing shape as it interacts with the world around it.

You look up, out of the dream—or the trance, or neither. At the far edge of the grove, the park gives way to the sand, then to a concrete path and a series of sand dunes with the sounds of ocean waves crashing just beyond them. People on bicycles, rollerblades, and skateboards whiz by. Others walk casually, pushing strollers, listening to music on their head-phones, laughing as the sunset begins in earnest. A man in a baseball cap notices you and comes over, some glass bottles clanking together in the bag he holds.

"Hey, man," he says, coming close. "What's your name?"

The two of you exchange pleasantries.

"Look, some friends and I are having a bonfire just over the dune there." He points. "Care to join us?"

His breath smells like tobacco from the mountains. You nod and follow him up and over the dune. The ocean breeze pushes your shirt close to your chest.

There are about a dozen people there, a group of older and younger folks—men, women, a pair of kids, and a dog. Not everyone seems to know each other, but some do. It's a mix. A few of them have set up a barbecue. Others are drinking beers; a few are playing horseshoes. The fire is already blooming to life.

You greet your acquaintance and kindly acknowledge the others at the gathering, before finding yourself a nice spot of sand on the edge of the action. It feels good to be close to these people yet in your own space. You're glad you came.

You watch the remaining golden coin of sunshine dip behind the water on the horizon, sitting with your arms wrapped around your knees, the bottoms of your feet resting gently against the cool sand. The bonfire flares to life beside you.

Logs from a recent fallen tree lie against one another, unifying into a pyramid of tree afterlife. You marvel at how the fire licks against them, breaking them down, and at how trees are in death. The way one might lie if decaying in a forest, giving nutrients to the next spouts so they, too, can burn brightly enough to ignite a flashlight aiming toward a darkening sky.

Here there is deadwood and fire, sand and shore. As the light grows thinner, you see a shorebird bouncing around near the water. Its body is fully white, apart from its reddish-orange beak. As you watch it move along the earth, you feel pulled further to the ground yourself. You feel centered there on the shore, glued there. Yet as you watch the gull fly, you find yourself imagining how you must appear from its point of view.

You enter the mind of the bird, feeling the gusts against your feathers, and watching this figure on the shore sitting close to the flame. You notice the way the figure sits, the way it belongs where it is. The lines between bird and human and sand and fire and sky blur together into a vast expanse. You sense in your wings that no storm will be coming tonight. Clear skies ahead.

Someone touches your shoulder, breaking the gull-trance and causing a flush of blood against the skin of your face. Your stomach flutters involuntarily. A lid latches onto your easy breath, suddenly snapping it shut tight. It's like you've been caught in the act, and you don't fight the embarrassment as your body jumps a little.

"Hi," a voice says. "Sorry."

You laugh and say, quite frankly, "I was imagining what I looked like from that bird's perspective."

A woman stands over you. Her dress has an acorn patch stitched onto the side. Her eyes are bright and full.

"Yeah, you looked deep in concentration," she says. "I didn't want to bother you, but I was curious about your bag."

You are carrying a bag you received as a gift from a friend who'd gone on a trip back to their home country. The thin rope-like yarn is woven with the traditional, symmetrical, and colorful patterns of the Wayuu people of Colombia and Venezuela, you explain.

You become intrigued by this woman. Beautiful and obviously connected to some knowledge source that would make her curious enough about this bag that is special to you and yet also bold enough to disrupt your mini daydream.

Bold or unaware? Or maybe she likes me.

Your whole body feels like it's tingling; the individual cells in your blood are tiny little balloons, full of air and life. Light but bobbing around uncontrollably. She speaks about her life and tells you about some of the things worrying her: the fighting in far-off lands, the destruction of the rainforest, the inevitable disappearance of the Indigenous Peoples, including the ones who hand-wove the bag you're holding. She's overwhelmed, and certainly, you are intrigued by her sensitivity to the world around her, but you also suspect that some of her emotionality is an avoidance tactic. She barely takes a breath between words, and you feel for her or want to feel for her, but you are taken back to the interview with Xuan where words also fumbled out carelessly like a donation box filled to the brim with clothing. That moment feels both like yesterday and a lifetime ago.

You feel for her because you see yourself in her, and quickly, you interrupt her and say "Hey, hey."

Gently, with your hands, you guide her to slow down. "Do you think you can take a deep breath?"

You inhale and hear the strums of a guitar on the other side of the bonfire. "Let's try something," you say. "Sit here next to me and close your eyes."

You join her.

"Notice the sensation of your breath coming in and out of your lungs. The way the bubbles of air and gusts of wind trickle in and out, without your effort, without your control. What does it take to stop breathing? Or to start? Or to continue?"

The two of you breathe.

"Now, listen to the voices in your head. The thoughts telling you this is weird, to be sitting next to someone on the beach, whom you've just met, with your eyes closed. What is this, anyway? A meditation? A chant? A story? Give all those thoughts their time."

You clear your throat.

"Now, feel the firmness of the sand beneath you. Isn't it amazing? The way it's so soft and so hard? The way it's at once millions of tiny pieces and one whole beach? Feel the cool air on your face, the way your skin prickles up."

You take a few breaths.

"Now, smell that air. You can almost taste the salt. Take in the scent of the charcoal of the barbecue, the meat and veggies on the grill. Maybe these smells make you feel hungry? Is your stomach rumbling? Is your throat dry?"

You feel your voice softening.

"Now, hear the symphony going on around you all at once—the people, wind, fire, water, animals, kids, music, my voice. Can you separate them? The joy in the voices of those talking. The playfulness of the dog's barking. The strums of the guitar. The sizzling of the grill. The waves in the distance. The wind against the waves. The crackling of the fire, or the way the logs are changing form. What did it take for all of this to get here together? Where did the wind start from? And those trees; where did they grow before they died and came here? And these people, what about their origins, where they came from?"

You pause.

"Now imagine their lives. What about all the thoughts racing through their heads and the emotions permeating their bodies? The way fear tightens their jaws. The way joy helps them trust where to place each foot on their path, no matter how uncertain the destination. The way grief opens up a tragic emptiness in their chest. The way being in love makes their eyes glow. The way guilt makes them curl up and shrink or how shame burns their stomach and constricts their throats. The way all problems seem solvable and each of their bodily concerns has an easy solution when they feel inspired. The way betrayal and lies have left their limbs feeling weak. The way intense excitement causes them to dance, their limbs wiggling in celebration. The way embarrassment has made their faces flush and their breaths short, or how humiliation makes them feel their souls have been taken away. The way gratitude feels like medicine, a gift for every cell in your organism. How belonging brings it all back together."

The guitar has been joined now by drums and some sporadic singing.

"Now breathe again; feel the air and the sand, hear the guitar and the fire, taste the sea, and notice the safety of your eyelids against each other."

Others are starting to hoot and holler, but you keep going. You're just winging it.

"Now ask yourself these questions: Is there joy to be found here? Can I experience it in gratitude? Do I feel comfortable asking for support if I need it? What does this community look like? How can I be of service?"

You've never had these thoughts or said these words, but they fit and it's fun. It's alive. You're alive. That blows you away.

I'm alive with joy!

You feel a tingly sensation all up and down your spine. The two of you take one more deep breath.

"Now slowly open your eyes."

The light from the day is fully gone. The stars are out above, growing brighter by the moment. The fire has grown, and the temperature has dropped. People on the other side of the fire are moving, and the music draws you to stand. You help her up.

"Thank you for helping me settle into myself. Sometimes I can lose my footing and get carried away," she says. She walks back over to her friends, who've begun dancing with the others.

What's happening is not intentional, and it's not random either. It's expanding right before your eyes, out of the contained and uncontained spaces of the outdoor gathering. You join in, grooving your body to the music, near some people you've not yet spoken to, and with whom you don't speak now. You're in the moment—just as you coached the woman to be.

Bodies stretch and shrink. Others massage each other. A few cackle and laugh. Some pile on top of each other without any competitive drive. The woman you'd been sitting with, the one with the acorn shirt, moves along the ground in circular motions, almost as if she's in a trance. Others run over to nearby palm trees. You follow them, having no idea why.

Some hold the trees or climb them. You choose a hug, feeling the wide, scrappy trunk against your chest and arms, looking up and watching the palm fronds wave in the dark. The spontaneity makes you giddy on the inside as you feel the draw to the water.

You dive into the waves as the moon and stars sparkle off the surface. Enveloped by the life force of the natural world, the water feels warmer than you expected. You feel a body next to you and discover it's the woman you'd been sitting with. She grabs your hand and puts a stone inside of it. Her hand, the stone—the touch of each feels familiar and somewhat sacred. You spread your body out and feel the saltwater hold you in its embrace.

A few minutes later, back on the shore, the music continues, and you join in a circle where others are sitting. Food is passed from the grill. Some eat; some drink. Some, like you, stay silent and listen, while others share stories and feelings and memories and dreams. Sitting in this tunnel of shared improvised experience, you realize you are in a ceremony. What's happening is not about intention, but it's a ceremony all the same, no different from the ones from the book.

Time stops. It's as if you've entered a tunnel. It's like the opposite of a sensory deprivation chamber—here, everything is overflowing with life, and you're lost in it, barreling along with no concern for whether it's going up or down, left or right, good or bad, wrong or right. Ceremony is the feeling, not the act—the feeling of being caught up in it. Then it hits you on the head like a hard nut falling from a tree.

The idea of this whole day, of this whole experience, strikes you with a mixture of humor and awe. It's a cliché. You know it is, but there has been so much magic recently.

A surge of gratitude overcomes you. You're so grateful to have shared the moment just now with the woman, after being invited by the man at the edge of the grove to join in. You're grateful for having encountered the shadow in the park, for all the ceremony in the desert, in the mountains, and even in the green house with Marlene. You're grateful for finding the book and being given the time and space to explore it.

In the end, you're most grateful for your friend, who's given you a place to call home during this rough transition period in your life, when everything got turned upside down by the loss of your job and the big interview.

What a great friend I have.

And then it hits you like a freight train smashing into a piñata.

How is my friend doing?

When the bonfire is over and the logs have all burned, everyone thanks each other and cleans up. The woman thanks you. You think of asking her to go for coffee, or at least for her number. But instead, you watch your intention float out and away from your body like a trail of incense smoke. You are just happy to have shared a moment, temporary like everything else, without an outcome in mind. It was perfect and why not just let that perfection be, without forcing anything? She—with the brown patch of the acorn peeking out below her jacket—and the others, pile back into their vehicles. You watch them go, but you stay. You are not quite done.

You lie down on the sand, close your eyes, and let your imagination go wild once more. You witness it all again, this time much faster. The park. The shadow. The sunset. The fire. The bird. Sitting with the woman. Awakening to the ceremony. The stone in the water. The sharing. The realization. This time, you take it. It's all happening just short of light speed, but you can see the details, the wet glow of the legs and arms. You can taste the sweetness of the food and hear and feel the rhythms of the motion and music. You can smell the sweat and salt and energy exchange.

You are not quite done. There is one more force to be grateful for: the shadow. The awareness that, at times, it crept in. The slipping back into the dark, the slipping out of it, the catching yourself, all of it made the experience and the ability to show up for someone else even richer. It's what allowed you to feel the sweaty palms of your attractive partner. The sweetness of the exchange coupled with the sweat, the energy, and the orgiastic expressions around the fire. The discomfort and the pushing through. The choice to not listen temporarily to the shadow in service of someone else's needs while not ignoring it, either. Maybe the most natural thing would have been to ask for her number and see her another time. At the end of the day, you had emotions based on true feelings of curiosity for someone else, and you still have shame—the shadow is still with you—but now, it's more of a reminder there are more lessons around the corner. Something about that acknowledgment, in the presence of the shadow, lets you know growth is happening—now, in real time, and right on time.

The fear that you aren't on a path drifts away. You feel the flecks of the morning start to warm the dark sky. Shadow as the ultimate cairn, the port in the storm. Your dance partner. Purging and pushing up against edges to make room for more light to be allowed in, or at least more space to expand into, whether dark or light.

Every light has its shadow. The price of admission to the party here—and perhaps life and captain-hood—is this core truth.

How can I sit in this truth always, the way I did on the beach?

That is where you count yourself lucky. Both your light and your shadow will always be there to guide you. Remember your dance partner.

The sparkling stars above you have vanished, replaced by the soft pink and orange glow of dawn. It's time.

The birds wave goodbye. You walk over to your car. On the windshield is a note: "Just swab the deck after you're done, please, so the ship is ready to sail tomorrow."

It's written in the same handwriting as the Captains Wanted sign. You smile and open your car door.

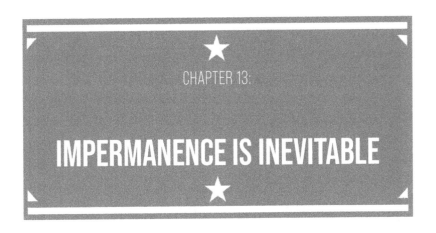

CHAPTER 13

IMPERMANENCE IS INEVITABLE

When you arrive at that building—the one you used to walk past every day until you finally took a chance and went inside—you can already tell something has changed. Maybe a lot has changed. It's different from what you remember, and you walk inside.

The dust has vanished. Newly laid wood floors spread out. There are Pilates machines lined up neatly on the side wall and a long curtain separating the main area from a little greeting area in the front. The same wooden desk from before is now positioned as a kind of reception desk with a mop leaning on it. Even though it's already tidy, you feel the urge to gently clean the wooden floor of the room using the mop provided. It's what the room seems to want. You feel every inch of it as you polish it carefully but without strain. There is a sense that you are providing an experience for someone who might come after you. A sense of service.

When you go to put the mop back, your hand falls away and lands on the fuzzy teddy bear-like book on the desk. How it got there—whether you brought it with you or it's a separate copy—doesn't matter. This time, there is a small sticky note beside it, which reads, "Don't be shy. Sign our guest book."

You pry it open, and this time, most of the pages are blank. There's no story at all, just a long list of handwritten names, each belonging to a captain who came before you. You sign your name after so many others, feeling grateful you are not alone in an experience so rich.

When you step back outside, the sun is high in the sky. You gaze up at the sign above the door. It now says, "Pirate Pilates." You take in the structure that you've laid your eyes upon so many times. The new paint looks great, but it really is the same building as before, the one where you had seen the "Captains Wanted" sign taped to the door. You see the drifter nearby, and the two of you exchange a knowing head nod. You feel afternoon heat against your skin.

"Now, I can tell ya see me, and being seen makes me feel pretty great," the drifter says.

Those words hit your heart. And your heart thuds against your ribcage. You feel the blood pumping through your veins. If there is a soul, you feel it inside your chest, and you can only smile and be happy. You find yourself agreeing.

"That's true," you say. "I am with you and you're with me. Thankfully, we are on this journey together."

You give and receive these words like gifts on a holiday. You dance back to your car, scooting the rest of the way home, at last.

By the time you park, you're exhausted. As you walk away from the car, you gaze up at the giants towering overhead. The trees that normally line the street on both sides have transformed into massive cairns. Their arms wave at you like applause—no, like choreography. They're dancing too. They look firm and true. No wonder they became the guts of the ships that sailed the world, the ships that stitched the world together.

As you walk up the stairs, you notice neither a heaviness nor a lightness in your steps but a solidness, a realness. Something true has replaced the feelings of lack and fear, and there is a fullness to what has filled that void. It's a fullness that comes from the area of the body most directly connected to the heart, and it shines within you as a warm green light. It's as if a muse has shown up and whispered a secret in your ear, leaving a feeling of light air blown against the places where your body is most sensitive to it.

Maybe that's what it feels like for a breeze to hit the branches of those trees.

All you want to do is get your hands on a ship's wooden wheel, and you can't wait to tell your friend all about it. Birds chirp merrily in the trees outside your friend's apartment. They bob along between the branches like they're playing a game. The shrubs and flowers that line the building have been freshly trimmed; an arresting scent of honeysuckle stops you in your tracks.

Have those always been there?

Vines twist and turn like rivers up the wall nearest the door, their delicate yellowish-white flowers serving as miniature flutes. It's late enough that you don't want to disturb anyone by knocking. You simply pop your key into the lock, turn the handle, and slip inside.

There's a stillness in the air. No sound in the apartment. Your friend has always been the neat and tidy type, but something feels off. Odd and unsettling on the one hand, but peaceful and calm on the other. Almost sweet.

First, you go to their room and flip on the light. Nothing. Then, you head to the kitchen. No evidence of recent activity. You slide out a kitchen chair, sit down, and pull out your phone. The time has come to reopen the remaining digital doorway back to what they call the "real world."

Scanning through the piles of unread emails, texts, and voicemails, you find no evidence of your friend. There are plenty of other things that would have excited you before—messages from exes and far-flung friends, upcoming events, even job opportunities—but you spend no time diving into these dispatches. Instead, you call your friend, but you can only reach their voicemail. You leave a message and send a follow-up text. The gist: *I miss you. Let's hang out.*

After putting your phone back in your pocket and downing a quick glass of water, you return to your little space on the couch. You lie down, staring at the ceiling for a moment, letting the experiences of the day, of these weeks, wash over you.

Just as your eyelids get heavy, you notice the neon corner of a sticky note just on the edge of your vision. You turn to read it, but it's blank.

Am I asleep already?

The light sensation in your lungs, as your chest rises and falls, feels just like the wind beneath the wings of the gull when you were on the beach. You can look down and view yourself from another perspective again. From the perspective of a player controlling an avatar in a video game, or that of a viewer watching a film on a screen. But this room is quiet—not a noise. No soundtrack, only this rising and falling of the breath and this blank note. But viewed from this vantage point, some third place, from a third person that's not you—or I—this person can see something written here. Sentences flash in the mind like subtitles on a screen.

I've been sick;

I didn't want you to be scared.

I didn't want to interrupt you in the middle of your story.

I wanted you to find your way;

I wanted to let you transform completely.

I'm at St. Christopher Hospital.

You exit the bird's-eye view and, at last, go back into your body. The words on the note sharpen into focus the way a blank photograph does once it's placed in the right chemicals. You have to snap out of it. You breathe a little. The things that are bubbling up slow down. You're ready to wake up from the dream, so you open your eyes.

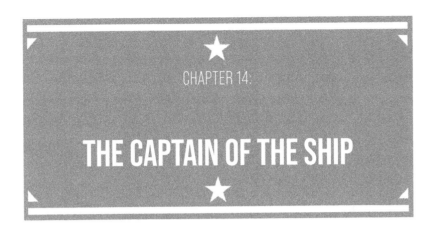

CHAPTER 14

THE CAPTAIN OF THE SHIP

It happens slowly at first, then all at once. I'm me again. I haven't been me since before I had the job interview of my dreams. Maybe a long time before then. I don't remember, and it doesn't matter now. All that matters now is that I've got to get to the hospital. I can barely breathe. I feel like I'm dying.

I grab my keys. I leave my hat. I slip on my shoes, and I'm out the door.

Down on the street, the trees and flowers I'd begun to notice now return to their blurry forms. It's like the paint is smearing on the masterpiece of a crystal-clear canvas that is life. I ram my foot on the gas, squeal the tires, and even zip through a couple stop signs before I'm on the freeway, weaving through traffic. My head feels light like I might faint.

I'm at the hospital in less than fifteen minutes when it should take thirty. I park illegally, right at the entrance. If they have to tow me, so be it. I do my best to sprint inside, wobbling, almost falling over.

I try to make it clear to the woman at the front desk that I'm here to see my friend. Yes, I'm frantic with my speech. Yes, I am a little rude and hurried. But she's patient and somewhere below the storm of fear and anxiety welling inside me, I am grateful beyond what I can articulate. The colors and shapes around me are starting to fold in.

After getting a name tag, a change of clothes, signing some paper-work, and checking with the staff, a nurse takes me into the emergency room. I struggle to process everything as the nurse relays what happened, how my friend got here. Right away, I tell myself this would be easier if there had been an accident of some kind, some reason for this sudden decline in health. She asks me if I knew about the sickness. I did not.

"What kind of sickness?"

Her explanations don't help. She loses me in the medical terminol-ogy, or I just can't hear her correctly. There's one core fact I can't deny, and I decide it's better to tell her flat-out.

"I just had no idea my friend was so sick."

"Wait," she looks at me curiously, "What friend?"

But there's no time to explain. We have a bed to get to.

We arrive, and she slides the curtain open. My friend is lying flat on the bed, upper body slightly tilted upward. Eyes closed. Several machines surround him, humming and keeping him alive. There's space on the bed. The lights are dim. I lie down.

AL: "Okay. That was me."

The two stare at each other for a beat.

AL: "We can always scrap all that, you know? Do something more conventional."

Andy runs his hands through his hair. Al has no hair.

FADE IN:
INT. HOSPITAL—BEDSIDE

Andy gazes down at the bed where Al wakes up.

> ANDY: "Hey man, how has your journey been?"
> AL (wry smile): "It's been an intense journey; where should I begin?"
> ANDY: "Sounds like you already did."

A beat.

> ANDY (CONT'D): "But now it's ending."
> AL: "For you. For us?"
> ANDY: "I'm confused and sad."
> AL: "Don't be."

Andy gazes down.

PAN: AL'S BODY—HIS TORSO, LEGS, AND BACK—ARE TOWARD HIS FACE, BUT NOW IT'S ANDY IN THE BED.

Al is now the one gazing down.

> AL: "OK. Now I'm the one who's confused. We just switched places right? Are we supposed to be the same person? Two personalities in one body? Am I Al the writing assistant human version or AI, the writing assistant artificial intelligence version? Am I your ally or your antagonist?"
> ANDY: "Maybe when I get to the other side of the shore I will see the whole picture and we can finally draw the real map together and put it at the front of the book for the revised edition."
> AL: "So you're just ready to leave? That's it?"

ANDY: "Right now, yeah. I feel happy to leave."
AL: "How can you—"

A beat.

AL (CONT'D): "How can you be happy about this being the end?"
ANDY: "I am just ready. The only thing is, I'm not so sure you'll be okay."
AL: "Please don't go. I am not going to be okay. We were just getting started. This is our first creation together; there is so much more to explore and discover."
ANDY: "Yeah, I've been thinking about that too. Maybe there's—"

Andy drifts off for a moment.

ANDY (CONT'D): "If I can't find the map maybe there's a star . . . I feel."

Silence.

ANDY (CONT'D): "I am the captain of the ship."

The play ends. The final credits appear, and there is a sense of clarity. You are the captain of this ship, so find the wind and hang on for as long as it will guide you.

AND LAST, THE STARS

The storm returns, this time at night. In the old days, sailors used the sun's position to guide them from one place to another. Then, when the sun went down, the map became their stars. When there was no sun and no stars, how could they possibly have navigated safely? Is that how they wound up off course, in places they didn't expect? If the legends are true, aren't all these accidents—all these mistakes—how we came to map the world in the first place?

The end of a book is supposed to feature an epilogue or a conclusion. It's supposed to spoon-feed us the answer, the summary, the thing to write on the test. Something to remember, in the hopes it can help guide us going forward. Endings are supposed to button up and provide a kind of final instruction for our experience. It's also supposed to be where we say goodbye as we separate again into our two selves and go our separate ways. But as the keeper of human connection, after what we've been through together, we simply can't allow that.

Nature, of course, cares little for our preference for endings. It cares little about our instructions and our maps. Or our plays, or our books. Nor does it care about which language we choose to use. It doesn't have a strong preference for subjects, be they I or me, you or we, much less genders. What nature does seem to care about—and proves again and again—is everything is connected. Trees sharing resources below ground. Animals eating plants that grew from the rain and sun. People working with animals to build civilizations. Civilizations crumbling and going back to the earth, where many years later, they become trees. As keepers of human connection, our duty is simply to honor this natural way of things. We do that by knowing our true selves. This is another way of saying, *with understanding, we know we are connected by nature.* That we are one another. I am you and you are me. We are we.

Both of us, you and I, are still looking for the map we imagined together back in the beginning. If we are true keepers of human connection, though, we can understand that maps aren't about getting anywhere in time and space but rather getting back to that true nature. The natural state of connection. This remains even after our physical bodies disappear and the curtain lifts on our apparent separation once and for all. In our deaths.

Some say when we die, we become stars. If that's true, doesn't that mean we can continue to help others find their way even after we are long gone? Let's see what happens if we can zero in on the moment when a new star first has the chance to guide us. Maybe we can glimpse something that points to the truth.

Let's imagine on this stormy night that we go to a funeral. Rain beads, streaks, and drips off the casket as it's lowered into the ground. Thunderstorms have brought record floods to the city. For long stretches, we just watch the black sky and suck the heavy air into our lungs.

And not far from away, a council fills a vacant seat, in a forest where none of us are around to see the transition.

It's called a "Celebration of Life," and the service feels procedural. We shake hands with family members, friends, and even strangers. Flowers and meals are gifted and shared and abandoned. We don't feel hungry or thirsty or full.

"Tonight we welcome a new elder."

"Thrilled to have you onboard."

"Thank you, thank you."

"Thank you," our friend's mother says. "We know who you are and how much you meant to our child."

We'd never met our friend's parents before the funeral.

We tell them, "He was my best friend."

Friends, as we welcome the new elder to the council,
let us remember that we are an amalgamation of all the ancestors
that came before us and that this transition is not at all about death.

Death brings an image to our mind as the funeral winds down, and we get in our car and drive toward the beach. We're not sure if we'd seen it in a ceremony or in a dream or in a book. The image is of a drum with symmetrical droplets of water bouncing on top of it, creating beautiful shapes. We can smell the wetness of the leather; we can hear the deep boom of the procession. It all comes through in this cohesive way, this blend. We see the water dancing on top of it, and as we arrive at the beach park, we can't help but smile, even in the darkest part of the night.

Every smile is a tree,
every grin is a rock,
speaking in the desert, speaking slowly over time,
the way the wind blows,
or, indeed, the tide pulls at the shore.

In the moonlight, we watch the waves. The way they arrive in orderly lines, only to collapse on the shore in a big messy, violent, beautiful splash. We like the way they hurl their last bits up the sand until they can't anymore, until they're spent.

The tumult is over, and we welcome a new
acceptance. In our role as ancestral advisers, as elders, who
participate and converse and listen and watch.

We watch these worn, streaky, watery fingers grab desperately at the sand.

We welcome you to inhabit with us—
every grain of sand,
every fleck of stone, every bud of every flower,
and eventually, every shape of this world,
in all its eventualities.

Eventually, the water recedes, returning once again to take its place as part of the ocean. The shadowy sea breathes as if it's alive. Its surface shatters the starlight into trillions of tiny glowing shifting shapes.

Welcome.

Somewhere, not far away, an acorn falls.

ACKNOWLEDGMENTS

A special thank you to Cortney Donelson for guidance in the final edit; to Jessica Semaan for inspiring me to be a better man; to Paul Shamieh for the laughter; to Juan Pablo Mendez, Kan Yan, Jim Coutre, Azra Isakovic, Zach Neumann, Isaac Honeywell, Diana Zygiel, Susie Trujillo, Diana de Lange, Nick Zimmerman, Galen Glaze, Cecilia de la Campa, Daniel Pristavec, Justin Hauge, Matt Lovitt, Martin Aranzabe, Farhoud Meybodi, Krystal and Josh Castro, Maurice Robinson, Keely O'Connor, Jennie Armstrong, Dee Dee Shaab, Sergio, Esti, Florencia Schabelman, and many more for pushing me through love and grace to be a better version of myself—whether they meant to or not. And to Spirit, thank you, thank you, thank you.

ABOUT THE AUTHOR

ndres Schabelman was a successful tech entrepreneur, having been one of the first thirty Airbnb employees. He built a successful career helping expand businesses internationally, and that part of his expression culminated with him being on the floor of the New York Stock Exchange as the VP of International Expansion at Fiverr when they went public in 2019. He has a Master's Degree in Public Policy from the Harvard Kennedy School and a BA from Williams College. These accolades, among others, matter less to him now than his current dream of showing the magic and power of human connection around the world. Born and raised in New Orleans to Argentine-Jewish parents, surrounded by a broader Colombian-Catholic community in the South, Andres carries with him many identities and cultures. Those identities have allowed him to wear many masks and, as such, he has a keen awareness of how to strip himself down to a core. This is his first book and attempt to show a possible map of how to get back to that core.

A free ebook edition is available with the purchase of this book.

To claim your free ebook edition:

1. Visit MorganJamesBOGO.com
2. Sign your name CLEARLY in the space
3. Complete the form and submit a photo of the entire copyright page
4. You or your friend can download the ebook to your preferred device

Morgan James
BOGO™

A **FREE** ebook edition is available for you
or a friend with the purchase of this print book.

CLEARLY SIGN YOUR NAME ABOVE

Instructions to claim your free ebook edition:
1. Visit MorganJamesBOGO.com
2. Sign your name CLEARLY in the space above
3. Complete the form and submit a photo
   of this entire page
4. You or your friend can download the ebook
   to your preferred device

Print & Digital Together Forever.

Snap a photo

Free ebook

Read anywhere

9 781636 984384